HOLDING HARPER

A WAVERLY WILDCATS NOVELLA

JENNIFER BONDS

This book is a work of fiction. Names, characters, places, and incidents either are the product of the author's imagination or are used fictitiously. Any resemblance to persons, living or dead, business establishments, events, or locales is entirely coincidental. The author acknowledges the trademarked status and trademark owners of various products referenced in this work of fiction. The publication and use of these trademarks is not authorized, associated with, or sponsored by the trademark owners.

Holding Harper: A Waverly Wildcats Novella

Copyright © 2020 by Jennifer Bonds. All rights reserved. No part of this book may be reproduced, scanned, transmitted, or distributed in any manner whatsoever without prior written permission from the author except in the case of brief quotations embodied in articles or review.

Edited by Lea Schafer
Cover Design by Jennifer Bonds
Cover Art from Deposit Photos
ISBN: 978-1-953794-03-1
First Edition 2020
www.jenniferbonds.com

1

HARPER

"I can't believe I let you talk me into this." I tug at the too short hemline of my scarf-turned-toga. The damn thing is short as hell and I'm pretty sure if I lift my arms, the guys of Sig Chi will be seeing a lot more than my butt cheeks.

Mom would be so proud.

"I can't believe we're going to a Sig Chi party," Bri whispers, vibrating with excitement. "Their parties are epic. I heard the campus police have to break them up at least once a month."

"All the more reason I should've stayed my ass at home to watch Netflix." I give my bestie the side-eye, but it's a wasted effort. Bri's a master of ignoring anyone or anything that dares stand between her and her goals, which tonight includes getting shit-faced with a bunch of over-privileged frat boys in togas.

"Spoilsport."

We all have that one friend. The one full of good intentions and bad ideas. You know, the one it's impossible to say no to? Brianna is totally that friend, and the more she talks, the more I'm convinced she's not going to let me graduate without spending at least one night in jail. Which I'm sure will look stellar on my resume.

"You need to live a little. It's senior year," Bri chides, looping her arm through mine, like she's afraid I'm going to make a run for it. "If ever there was a time to cut loose, this is it."

"Says the girl who's not starting clinical rotations on Monday."

I adore Bri—the girl is made of awesome—but as a Family and Consumer Sciences major, she just doesn't understand my workload. Waverly's nursing program is no joke and I'm hanging by a thread. I don't have time for frat parties and hangovers. Not when I'm short on clinical hours. The fall semester doesn't even start for another three weeks, but since I need to make up hours, my advisor arranged for me to start rotations early.

Lucky me.

"Whatever." Bri drags me up the sidewalk that leads to the Sig Chi house. A loud bass spills from the front door of the big brick McMansion, but with most of Waverly's students on summer break, it doesn't seem too wild. Not yet, anyway. "How do I look?"

"You know you look hot." I nudge her shoulder playfully. With her petite frame, sun-kissed skin, and silky black curls, she's rocking her toga—which covers a whole lot more skin than mine. "You've got this."

Bri's been nursing a crush on one of the Sigs since sophomore year, so even though I'd rather be curled up at home in something with an elastic waistband and no bra, here I am.

"You look pretty damn good yourself," Bri says, as we climb the steps to the front porch.

"I look like I should be wearing seashells and a mermaid tail," I scoff, pointing to the flaming red wig on my head.

"You said you didn't want to be recognized and now you won't be. You're welcome." She smiles impishly. "Besides, I don't think they make seashells in your size."

She's not wrong. Where Bri is all sharp angles and angelic

grace, I'm tall and curvy with the kind of rack that gets more looks than *Cosmo*. Fortunately, I grew up in a family of strong women, and while there are days I wish I had Bri's B-cups, I'm proud to say I'm comfortable in my own skin. After all, why go through life wishing you were someone else?

"God, I wish I had your boobs," Bri says, staring forlornly at my chest.

Case in point.

"They're all yours as long as you take the backaches and leering stares too," I offer, shooting her a wicked grin.

Bri scrunches up her nose in distaste. "Hard pass."

We collect red plastic cups from the guy at the door and make our way down the paneled hall to the dimly lit living room. The house is stifling, no thanks to a recent heat wave, and a fine sheen of sweat is already coating my hairline from the walk over.

Good thing I'm not trying to impress anyone.

Senior year is rumored to be hell for nursing students and I have zero time for distractions, especially those of the male variety.

In the living room, most of the furniture has been pushed up against the wall to create a small dance floor where sweaty coeds in ill-fitting sheets grind against one another. I scan the room, searching for a familiar face, but all I see are flushed cheeks and way too much skin. There's a beer pong table set up in the corner, made from—what else—an unhinged door.

Bri makes a beeline for the keg, and I'm close on her heels. I'm not a fan of cheap beer, but it's eleventy billion degrees and I'm not about to turn down a cold drink.

A guy in a SpongeBob toga smiles as we approach, and he offers to fill our cups. Unfortunately, his ability to multitask is nonexistent. He's so busy staring at Bri that he overfills her cup and beer sloshes to the already sticky floor.

"What the fuck, Jones." Adam, Bri's crush, appears at her side and takes over the tap. "Amateur."

Bri laughs and he flashes her a dimpled grin. With any luck, Adam will finally get his head out of his ass and ask her out on a real date, making my first trip to Greek Row my last. Probably wishful thinking, but a girl can dream, right?

Adam fills our cups and after a few minutes of small talk, he asks Bri to dance, so I do what any good wing woman would do, and offer to hold her beer.

#ThirdwheelFTW.

I sip my beer—which is lukewarm—and drift toward the back wall, where I have a decent shot of blending in with the furniture. The music is so loud I can hardly think, and when the song changes for the third time and Bri makes no move to leave the dance floor, I realize I'm in for a long night. I resign myself to people watching, taking in the rainbow of togas, and when my cup is empty, I start in on Bri's.

The way she's grinding on Adam, I doubt she'll care.

I'm halfway through her beer when a cute guy in a crisp white toga approaches. We're around the same height—five-nine—and he's got neatly trimmed chestnut hair, hazel eyes, and nice teeth. I've always had a thing for guys with nice teeth, but there's something about him that's almost *too* perfect.

Hell, he reminds me of a Ken doll I had when I was nine.

"Having fun?" he asks, flashing the Sig Chi pin on the knot of his toga.

Eww. Douchey frat bro is so not a good look.

"Sure."

"I haven't seen you around the Sig house before," he says, gaze fixed on my chest. *And there you have it, folks. All plastic, no substance.* "I'd definitely remember if we'd met before."

More like he'd remember my boobs.

"I'm Chris." He leans in to close the gap between us.

Granted, it's loud, but his lips damn near brush the shell of my ear when he asks, "And you are?"

Totally grossed out.

"Ariel."

He pulls back and his eyes go wide, like he's ninety-nine percent sure I'm bullshitting him. Still, he goes with it. "What's your major, Ariel?"

"Nursing." Maybe if I keep it short, he'll get the hint and move on.

"Nice." He bobs his head appreciatively. "I'm pre-med."

I sip my beer, but say nothing, determined to stick with my *do not engage* plan.

"All right, Ariel." He skims his fingers down my bare arm, sending my creep alarm into overdrive. "I can tell you're not into the usual bullshit, but since we're both going to be in the medical profession, how about we go up to my room and study some anatomy?"

He stares at me expectantly, and it's all I can do not to throw up in my mouth.

What. An. *Ass.*

"Oh, sweetie." I flash him a saccharine smile. "We don't need to go anywhere for me to recognize a bad case of micropenis." I glance down, staring at the spot where his cock should be. "You've got all the symptoms: inflated ego, short stature, douchey pickup lines."

His jaw goes slack and anger darkens his eyes before he snaps his mouth shut. He mutters something that sounds a lot like *sea witch* as he turns on his heel and storms off.

Ariel 1, Frat Bro 0.

"Damn, Red. That was savage."

I turn slowly, taking in the beefy dude to my left. How long has he been standing there and how the hell did I miss him before? The guy must move like a ninja, which is impressive given he's got a few inches on me. He crosses his thick arms over his chest and stares down at me, Nordic eyes dancing with laughter.

"Remind me never to piss you off."

I shrug and lift my chin. "He's the one who wanted to discuss anatomy. It's not my fault he didn't like the diagnosis," I say, doing my best to ignore his brilliant smile. *No time for hookups. Not even if he's got the world's most perfect teeth.* "Honestly, he's lucky I didn't give him a complimentary kick in the balls to go with it."

He laughs and shakes his head, an unruly blond wave flopping down over his right eye. He drags a hand through his hair, pushing it back, but with the humidity, it's a futile effort. "Just as well. You'd be wasting your time with a guy like that."

I arch a brow. "Really?"

I mean, he's not wrong, but who is he to weigh-in on my nonexistent love life?

"Absolutely." He smirks, riding the razor-sharp line between confident and cocky. "It's easy to appreciate a beautiful woman. But it takes a real man to appreciate a beautiful, confident woman who can take care of herself."

A warm flush spreads across my chest. He thinks I'm beautiful?

So not the point, Harper.

"Um, thanks." Because, yeah, that was probably the best compliment I've ever received. After all, what woman doesn't want to be respected for being confident and self-sufficient? Hell, most of the guys I know are intimidated by strong women.

Just another reason to avoid dating until after graduation.

He takes a long slug from his water bottle and I watch in fascination as his throat bobs, the corded muscles of his neck rippling seductively. My pulse flutters and I glance down at my red plastic cup, which is mostly empty now.

Time to lay off the beer, because throats? Not supposed to be sexy.

He flashes me a knowing grin. "I take it you're not part of the Greek scene?"

"Nope." I turn to search the writhing crowd for Bri. I need to get out of here before I do something stupid like throw my panties at this unicorn. Because *of course* the universe would tempt me with the only enlightened male on campus when I'm already behind on life. "I guess you could say I'm popping my Greek Row cherry tonight."

Oh. My. God.

As soon as the words are out of my mouth, I realize what I've said. And that flush on my chest? Yeah, it's scorching up my neck and across my cheeks like a five-alarm blaze.

"Okay, that sounded bad," I stammer, resisting the urge to fan my face. "I didn't mean—"

"It's all good." He chuckles and it's...nice, the sound rich, warm, and unreserved. "I know what you meant, Red."

"Quit calling me Red."

"Well, I'm sure as shit not calling you Ariel." He quirks a brow and stares pointedly at my fake hair. "Red suits you, but I'd much prefer your real name."

Busted.

"I'll tell you what," he says, pitching his voice low. His eyes lock on mine and there goes my stupid heart again, fluttering like a hummingbird on Red Bull. "Dance with me and afterward, if you don't want to tell me your name, no hard feelings."

"Pass. I don't dance." I give him another once-over. My short-ass toga has nothing on his, which is bordering on indecent. "Besides, I'm pretty sure you're one song away from flashing your bits to the entire house."

Not that I don't appreciate the view, because I hate sculpted pecs, six-pack abs, and thick thighs...*said no woman ever.*

"I like to show off my legs." He smirks again, and damn if it doesn't suit him. "They're one of my best attributes."

Yes, yes they are.

And there's no harm in looking, right?

"I'm not one to push my company on a woman, Red, but I'll be right over there,"—he points to the beer pong table—"if you change your mind."

"I won't." I don't know which one of us I'm trying to convince, but even I'm not buying that line.

"Fair enough." He shrugs, a smile pulling at the corner of his lips. "I'm going to walk away now, but don't think I won't know if you're staring at my second-best asset."

He turns, and wouldn't you know it? I find myself doing just that, the white sheet pulled tight across the firm muscles of his ass for my viewing pleasure.

2

CHASE

Several of my teammates slap me on the back and offer fist bumps as I join the crowd at the beer pong table. Reid and Coop, Waverly football's biggest bromance, are facing off against a couple of Sigs. One of the guys offers me a beer, but I decline, holding up my nearly empty water bottle.

"I'm driving." Mainly because my scholarship doesn't cover summer expenses like food and lodging. Not that I'm complaining. My parents' place is only a thirty-minute ride from campus, so I can still use the university football facilities—which are far superior to anything my hometown gym offers—over break.

Besides, I don't need to get wasted to have a good time.

Of course, I'd be having a better time if I were dancing with Red, her electric-blue eyes locked on mine, her curves hugging my body in all the right places. And the way she told off that Sig without batting an eyelash? That shit had me hard as steel. I resist the urge to turn and find her in the crowded living room. The last thing I want to do is come off like a stalker, but damn, I hope she changes her mind about that dance.

I can't remember the last time a woman captivated me so thoroughly.

Probably never.

Which is why I'm not leaving until I get her name.

"Ready for training camp?" Reid, our team captain and star quarterback, asks.

"Ready for a national title," I shoot back as he sinks a ball into one of the Sigs' cups. "You?"

"Hell, yeah!" he roars. "We're going all the way this year. I can feel it."

Reid and I aren't close, but he's got a hell of an arm, and he's going to be a good captain. All the guys on the team respect him. Even those of us on Special Teams, who are used to being left out in the cold when shit goes wrong. I don't envy Reid the pressure of his position, but being a kicker isn't much better.

No matter how hard you train, you're only as good as your last kick.

A few of the other guys join in and we talk football as Reid and Coop decimate the Sigs, along with the next two challengers.

Training camp starts in a week, and I'm more than ready to get down to business. It's been too long since Waverly won a national championship and for those of us who won't be playing ball professionally, it's our last chance to be part of something great. Hell, having a shot at a national title was the whole reason I came to Waverly in the first place.

That and a free ride to a college degree.

"We need more beer," Coop announces, holding a pitcher upside down, as if to prove it's empty.

"I've got you." I grab the empty pitcher because I'm a team player and being beer bitch will give me an excuse to check on Red.

I squeeze through the crowd of sweaty bodies, and the closer I get to the speakers, the greater the vibrations rattling through my body.

Jesus. It's a wonder these guys haven't blown out their eardrums.

There's no sign of Red, and when I get to the keg, it's kicked. I'm 0-2 and frustration's burning in my gut when a drunk guy in a SpongeBob toga tells me there's another keg on the front porch.

Too late to get the girl, but I can still get the beer.

I make my way outside, where it's about ten degrees cooler. The porch is dark, but I find the keg easily enough. I'm nearly done filling my pitcher when there's a commotion on the lawn.

"If you idiots don't give me back my shoes, I swear to God..."

What the hell?

Red?

I abandon the keg and slam the pitcher down on the porch railing.

"Don't be like that," a male voice teases. "We're just playing."

Molten lava courses through my veins, hot and caustic. I'm down the steps like a shot, scanning the yard for Red.

If those drunk assholes laid one finger on her...

Relief crashes over me like a tidal wave when I spot Red, barefoot in the grass and seemingly unharmed. She's standing between two Sigs, hands planted on her curvy hips. I watch in disbelief as one of the jackasses tosses a strappy leather sandal to the other like some goddamn game of monkey in the middle.

"What the fuck is going on out here?" I clench and unclench my fists, heart pounding like I'm about to take the field and the game's on the line.

"I took my sandals off for a few minutes and these idiots,"— Red stabs a finger at the kid in front of her—"confiscated them and threw one of them up on the roof."

Not cool, but not as bad as it sounded. Not by half.

I exhale slowly, blowing my breath out through my nose. The idea of these guys—of anyone—hurting her burns like acid in my gut. I need to focus on something else, anything else, to erase those images from my mind. "Why did you take your shoes off? That house is filthy. I don't even want to think about the shit you could catch going barefoot."

Red huffs, her breasts rising and falling emphatically as she rolls her eyes. "My feet were killing me. And if you must know, I took them off outside."

I shake my head in disbelief. "I will never understand why women wear those torture devices you call shoes."

"They're cute," she fires back, turning that sexy sarcasm my way.

"You know guys don't give a shit what you wear on your feet, right?"

Which is the wrong thing to say—*obviously*—but my brain's still trying to process the fact that she's okay, while my body wants to pound the guys hassling her.

Red looks down her nose at me, gaze as fiery as her hair. Turns out she's even hotter when she's mad. "You know women don't wear cute shoes to impress guys, right?" She sniffs and crosses her arms over her chest, making her full breasts swell. "And you know what? I'm done discussing my life choices. I just want to get my shoe and go home."

Right. The shoe.

"Where is it?" I demand, turning to Tweedledum and Tweedledumber.

They exchange a look and start giggling like a couple of third graders. "Like she said, it's on the roof."

I rake a hand through my hair, swallowing my frustration.

Watching these rich pricks, who've never had to work—or want—for anything, strut around like the kings of campus leaves a bad taste in my mouth.

"What's the big deal?" Tweedledumber asks.

"The big deal," I say through gritted teeth, "is this is no way to treat a guest, especially a lady."

"Oh, my God." Red presses the tips of her fingers to her temples. "This is what I get for hanging out on Greek Row."

"What?" I ask, taken aback by her tone. "I'm just trying to help."

She gives a sexy little snort. "If you want to help, get my freaking shoe down."

"Yeah." Tweedledum elbows his buddy in the ribs. "Go up there and get the lady's shoe."

I glare at the shoe-stealing idiots. They're either too drunk or too stupid to realize I'm about three seconds from losing my shit, so I turn on my heel and do the only thing I can think of. I jog up the front steps and hop onto the stone railing that encompasses the wide front porch. I do a quick balance check and reach for the roof. It's just out of my grasp, but I can reach it easily if I jump.

So I do.

My fingers latch onto the roof's edge and I pull myself up, muscles straining at the weight of my suspended body.

Damn, I hate pull-ups.

Once my chest is over the lip of the roof, I sling a leg over, using the leverage to pull the rest of my body up. I'm just climbing to my feet when my teammates spill out of the house, looking for the pitcher of beer I was supposed to deliver.

There's a heated discussion, but I block it out, focusing instead on my next move.

The porch roof is large and flat, spanning the entire width of the house. I do a quick inspection—no sandal to be found—and turn my attention to the steel drainpipe bolted to the side of the house. I give it a tug, confirming it's solidly attached.

I crack my neck and roll my shoulders as I consider the climb.

"Spellman, get your ass down here," Reid barks. "As your team captain, I am telling you this is a bad fucking idea!"

"I have to agree with el capitán," Coop drawls. "Forget the shoe. These assholes will buy the lady a new pair."

It's that easy for them. They've probably never had a problem that couldn't be solved by throwing money at it.

"Don't tell us you're afraid of heights," one of the drunk Sigs taunts.

"I'm not afraid of anything," I bite out, too low for them to hear.

Rich pricks. If Coop wasn't a member of the frat, I'd never show my face on Greek Row. Not that it matters, because no way in hell am I backing down. The evolved part of my brain tells me I have nothing to prove, but the caveman part, the part that drives me to grind and hustle every day, tells me to get my ass up there and make those assholes eat their words.

The two drunk idiots start laughing and there's a quiet thump followed by muttered curses. I don't know what's going on down there, but I'd like to believe Coop slapped one of those jackasses in the back of the head.

"Your friend is right," Red calls, words high and tight. Maybe it makes me an asshole too, but my chest warms at the concern in her voice. "My shoe is not worth it."

I pause my drainpipe inspection and glance down at Red, drinking in the miles of creamy skin and the way her blue eyes sparkle in the moonlight. "No worries. I've played so much Donkey Kong, I'm like a spider monkey. I'll be up and back in no time."

"And we'll all be down here looking up your skirt," Coop hollers.

I give him the finger and start my climb, gritting my teeth as my knuckles scrape against the house's brick exterior.

Worth it if I get Red's number.

Shimmying up the drainpipe is harder than I expected, but I inch my way up, ignoring the comments from below. Someone's got their phone out, recording the whole thing, and the blinding light is pointed right at me.

Shit. If Coach finds out about this, I'll be running lines until I puke.

No time to worry about that now. I reach the top of the drainpipe and spot the shoe to my left. Thank Christ for small favors. At least I won't have to scale the roof.

If I can just reach it...

I lean toward the sandal, keeping my right hand wrapped firmly around the drainpipe. The tips of my fingers brush the soft leather, but I can't quite get a grip on it. Using my feet, I push myself a little farther up the drain and try again.

The pipe groans under my weight, but I manage to hook a finger through one of the straps and pull it back.

Score!

I hold up my trophy and the crowd below goes wild. Red smiles up at me like I'm a freaking hero and I know without a doubt that I'm getting her number tonight.

Just as I'm about to toss the shoe down, the drain groans ominously. I reach for the lip of the roof, but it's too late. The pipe breaks free of the house, sending me careening backward.

Oh, shit.

There's a high-pitched scream as I sail through the air, and then everything goes black.

3

HARPER

TGIF. I force a smile that feels more like a grimace as I approach the nurse's station. The first week of clinicals has been hell and the weekend can't get here fast enough. The nurse I'm assigned to shadow is a real-life Nurse Ratched. Demanding, no nonsense, and completely void of patience. Which is sort of understandable since this is a teaching hospital and she's got a revolving door of inexperienced future RNs to train, but that's hardly a comfort when my feet are swollen and I only got four hours of sleep last night.

I'm literally running on coffee and fear of failure at this point. Just counting down the hours until I can put my feet up and relax for one glorious day. Or, more likely, put my feet up and study. Because if this week's taught me anything, it's just how much I still have to learn before graduation.

It's karma kicking your ass for the Sig Chi party.

Bile burns the back of my throat and I close my eyes, stuffing down the guilt. Yes, I told that guy to go get my shoe. Yes, he turned out to be Waverly's starting kicker. And yes, his broken leg has him benched for the season. But it's not like I was the one who dared him to climb up on that roof.

Not that it makes me any less responsible.

So much for do no harm.

"You're late, Miss Payne," trills Nurse Ratch—Rogers. In addition to being a tyrant, she insists on formality. No first names in the surgical unit. Like this place isn't sterile enough with its stark white walls, fluorescent lights, and the overwhelming tang of disinfectant. Nope. We're all Miss Payne or Mr. Sanders, which is ridiculous considering we are literally up to our elbows in needles, blood, and human excrement.

I'm about to point out that my shift doesn't start for another three minutes, but I bite my tongue. No need to wake the beast this early in the day. "I'm sorry." I dip my head, doing my best to look contrite. "It won't happen again."

"We've got a new patient from SICU," she says, gesturing for me to follow as she marches down the hall. A transfer from the Surgical Intensive Care Unit? Must be a step-down case, then. My palms begin to sweat as I chase after her, Crocs squeaking loudly in the quiet hall. I've only dealt with standard pre- and post-surgical care, which means this patient is sure to be more challenging and probably has a more complicated history.

Inhale confidence, exhale doubt.

Right. This is what I've trained for. I've got this.

Although it's barely seven o'clock, the blinds are open when we enter the patient's room. Early morning sunlight spills across the foot of the bed closest to the window and cartoons are blasting from the TV. I'm one step behind Nurse Rogers as she introduces herself, and when she steps aside, I get my first look at the patient.

Broad shoulders. Wavy blond hair. Glacial blue eyes even a Norse god would envy.

My heart stutters.

No. Freaking. Way.

It's him. The guy from the party. The one who fell off the roof attempting to retrieve my shoe.

Nurse Rogers introduces me, probably giving the usual spiel about student nurses, but I don't hear any of it because Chase Spellman is my newest patient.

Karma, you dirty bitch.

Chase turns his attention to me and my heart leaps into my throat. *Shit.* What if he recognizes me? No, that's stupid, right? It was dark, and I was wearing that ridiculous wig. Plus, we never even exchanged names, even though I'd wanted to. If things had gone differently, I'd have happily traded my number for my sandal. The guy earned it after scaling the house like freaking Spiderman.

But that's out of the question now.

Just. Be. Cool.

"Seriously?" He flashes that panty-melting grin, and, I'm not going to lie, my pulse flutters. Just a little. Then my gaze shifts to his left leg, which is heavily bandaged and encased in a bulky metal brace. No, not a brace, an external fixator with metal pins that pierce the skin to hold broken bones in position. All thoughts of romance are quickly replaced with gut-clenching horror. "Your name is Nurse Payne?"

Heat blazes across my cheeks, but I clear my throat and nod. Because, yeah, no words.

"I hope it's not a portent of things to come." He rubs the back of his neck and chuckles, a deep, sexy rumble that raises goose bumps on my arms. "I gotta tell you, I was sort of hoping the worst of it was behind me."

For someone with a broken leg, he sure has a lot of jokes.

"I'm..." I clear my throat again, forcing confidence into my words. "I'm sure it is."

For him, anyway. Me? Not so much.

Waverly football has a passionate fan base and thanks to my

role in Chase's injury, I'm currently the most hated woman on campus. There's been speculation that the loss of the starting kicker could cost Waverly their shot at a national title and the fans are out for blood.

Mine.

Thank God no one but Bri knows I'm the infamous redhead from the video.

I just have to make sure it stays that way.

Which means I need to keep my mouth shut, even if the guilt is coiled around my heart like barbed wire. Chase cannot know I was the one at the frat house last weekend. Because if he did? He'd hate me, just like everyone else. And the thing is, I couldn't even blame him. If it weren't for me, he'd be at training camp with the rest of the team, chasing a national title, not lying here with a broken leg, a staggering number of get well cards, and floral arrangements his only company.

"An optimist." Chase nods in approval. "I like that."

"Don't worry," Nurse Rogers says, tapping away at the computer as she pulls up Chase's records. "We're going to take good care of you. You'll be back on your feet in no time."

"I'm going to hold you to that." Chase winks and I swear to God the old battle-ax smiles in return.

Seriously?

I blink—to make sure I'm not hallucinating—but no, she's smiling all right.

Figures. Even Nurse Rogers isn't immune to his charm.

"Miss Payne," she says, voice sharp, all business now. "Please take the patient's vitals while I review his charts."

My belly plummets and I nod, unable to force words past my lips.

I quickly wash my hands at the tiny sink near the door. Although my back is to Chase, I can feel his eyes on me as I move around the room, and it's disconcerting as hell.

Start with the easiest task first.

I grab the thermometer off the cart. Chase is sitting up, so contact will be minimal, but that doesn't stop my hands from shaking as I approach the bed.

"I'm going to start by taking your temperature," I explain, pleased the words come out cool and clinical. I've taken patient vitals so many times this week, I've lost count. Chase is no different. I just have to stay focused.

Which proves easier said than done.

Because no matter what I tell myself, Chase isn't like my other patients. The guy's a walking orgasm, all sexy confidence and irresistible charm. Which is ridiculous. I mean, who looks this good in a faded hospital gown anyway?

They definitely didn't teach this at nursing school.

His gaze travels over my body, leaving a trail of fire in its wake, before landing on my mouth. The corner of his mouth twitches, and I resist the urge to lick my suddenly dry lips. I gently slide the thermometer into his ear, pretending I don't notice his evergreen scent, which is a welcome change from the smell of disinfectant.

"Ninety-nine point eight," I announce when the thermometer beeps.

"I always run hot," he says, voice husky as his eyes lock on mine.

Is he... Is he actually *flirting* with me? In front of my supervisor?

"I can see that." Nurse Rogers punches his stats into the computer. "But we want to keep a close eye on it. We don't want your infection coming back."

"Infection?" I echo.

"Mr. Spellman took quite a nasty fall. He's got a concussion and underwent two surgeries in SICU." Nurse Rogers frowns at something on the screen. "The first to set the bones with plates and screws. The second to remove infected tissue, which is why he'll be staying with us for another week."

Chase's comments about the filthy frat house flash back to me and my stomach tightens.

"What type of break?" I ask, fighting to keep my emotions—and, okay, my guilt—in check. Technically, I already know the answer. I've been following the story in the news, but it's an expected question.

"Compound fracture of the tibia and fractured fibula."

Chase smirks, those beautiful blue eyes of his dancing with mischief. "My parents taught me to never do anything halfway."

"They must be so proud," I return without thinking, as I dispose of the probe cover on the thermometer and slip it into my pocket.

He chuckles and Nurse Rogers clears her throat, a not-so-subtle warning.

Right. Not only will she be grading my practical knowledge, she'll be advising my clinical instructor on my bedside manner.

"I'm going to take your pulse now," I tell Chase, reaching for his wrist. Technically, we have a Dinamap to take patient vitals, but Nurse Rogers is old-school and insists I prove my capability before I'm allowed to use the machine. "Just try to relax."

Chase quirks a brow and I just know he's itching to make a smartass comment, but he remains silent as I press two fingers to his wrist, just above the radial artery. I check my watch and when the second hand reaches twelve, I begin to count the beats.

One, two, three...

His skin is hot to the touch. Not burning up so much as welcoming, the kind of heat you want wrapped around you on a cold winter night when the snow is piling up and there aren't enough blankets in the world to keep you warm.

Eighteen, nineteen, twenty...

My gaze drifts and I find myself tracing the sharp line of his jaw, which is covered in golden stubble. I've always preferred clean-shaven guys, but he wears it well and for an instant—just one—I wonder what it would be like to kiss a guy with facial hair.

Thirty-one, thirty-two, thirty-three...

We're so close I can see the white flecks that circle his irises, reflecting the light like tiny chips of ice. Our eyes meet and my breath hitches in my throat.

Forty-seven, forty-eight, forty-nine...

Shit. We're too close. He's going to recognize me and then he'll hate me, just like the rest of the world. The idea guts me. I'd much rather—

"Heart rate?" Nurse Rogers asks, snapping me out of my head.

I glance down, trying to remember the count, but it's no use. I've lost it. "I'm going to take it again," I say, cheeks hot. "Just to double check."

I start again, this time pointedly ignoring Chase—*the patient's*—heated stare. I finish taking his vitals with record speed and I'm beyond ready to move on to the next patient once we've finished administering his meds.

Unfortunately, Nurse Rogers must not feel the same because she's unusually obliging as she checks his IV. "Is there anything else you need?"

I make the mistake of looking at Chase, and once again, his gaze is locked on me as he grins and says, "I've got everything I need."

4

CHASE

It's been a rough week, but things are finally looking up. Maybe a smoking-hot nurse is just what the doctor ordered. I'd much rather soak up Nurse Payne's sexy vibe than spend another day watching cartoons and wallowing in self-pity, wondering what my future holds.

Coach promised to hold a spot for me on next year's roster—after he ripped me a new one for being an irresponsible dumbass—but with two broken bones and the complications from the infection, who knows if I'll ever be able to play ball again?

Fear snakes up my spine and sweat beads along my hairline, a visceral reminder of my stupidity.

It's not like I was headed to the NFL, but I thought I had one more season. One more shot at a national title. Football's always been a means to an end for me. Play ball, earn scholarship money. But now that it's been ripped away?

That shit hurts.

Turns out the game—and the team—mean more to me than I'd realized.

The idea of never playing again, of never stepping out on

that field with my team... It's too much to wrap my head around. Hell, I'm still reeling from the prospect of spending two months on my ass. Doc says I can't put any weight on my leg for eight weeks.

Eight. Weeks.

It's only day six, and I'm already losing my mind.

The lead nurse is tapping away on the computer again, whispering instructions to Nurse Payne. I don't know what they're discussing, but I'm not going to complain about being left out. Not when it gives me a chance to study Nurse Payne's killer curves.

Look, I know scrubs aren't supposed to be sexy, but this girl? She's the exception. The navy fabric hugs her body, highlighting every dip and swell. Her dark hair is pulled back in a low ponytail that hangs over her shoulder, accentuating the most intense blue eyes I've ever seen. Plus, she's got these full, heart-shaped lips that are just begging to be kissed.

I feel like we've met before, but I can't seem to place her, so it's probably wishful thinking. Because if we'd met on campus? I definitely would've asked her out.

The lead nurse pulls out her phone and glances at the screen. "Finish up here. I'll be right back."

Nurse Payne's eyes go wide with panic, and for a second I think she's going to cut and run, but she holds her ground.

The lead nurse disappears into the hall and we're left alone.

I'm tempted to ask if it's her first day, because while her touch is gentle, her bedside manner? Well, let's just say I'm glad she's not holding a needle.

"So, you're a student at Waverly?" I ask, hoping to put her at ease.

"Yeah." She scans the room, looking everywhere but at me. Which kind of sucks, if I'm being honest. I thought we had a moment before.

"Me too. Or, at least, I was."

She freezes, then slowly turns to face me. "Was?"

"I had to withdraw for the semester." I point to my leg, which looks like something out of a sci-fi movie. Thank God for painkillers and the miracles of modern medicine, because if it felt even half as bad as it looked, I'd be wailing like a newborn.

Nurse Payne's brows knit in confusion. "Can't you do online classes?"

"No football, no scholarship." It's something no student athlete likes to think about, especially ones like me who are hustling to be the first college graduate in the family.

"I'm so sorry," she whispers, the color draining from her rosy cheeks.

Way to be a downer, Spellman.

"No need to apologize," I say hastily, feeling like a jerk. I'd been trying to loosen her up, not bring her down. The last thing I want is her pity. "It's not like you're the one who dared me to climb up on the roof, right?" She stiffens and presses her lips flat. "Besides, the doc says with a few months to heal and a little PT, I'll be back in cleats in no time."

Whether I'll be able to kick at the Division 1 level remains to be seen.

Fear rattles my chest, but I ignore it, focusing on the here and now. No sense sweating the future, not when I've got a beautiful woman to keep me company.

"That's good news," she says, busying herself at the medical cart. "You'll get the best possible care here. It may be a teaching hospital, but WUMC is one of the top-ranked hospitals in the state."

"So I've heard." I grin. "I was actually born here."

Her head pops up at that. "You're a local?"

"More or less," I admit, scratching the back of my head.

Damn, I need a proper shower. I'll need to ask about that later. "Born and raised in a tiny little town about thirty miles north."

I don't mention that Millheim is practically a one-road town or that my parents barely eke out a living running the local hardware store. She doesn't need all the gory details, and I have no interest in seeing that pitying look on her face again. I've worked too long, fought too hard to prove myself at Waverly. I'm not going to let this setback screw it all up.

"I'm from out east. Near Philly."

I cringe. "Please don't tell me you're an Eagles fan."

"Let me guess." She smirks. "You're a Steelers fan?"

"Hell, yeah." My dad and I watched the Steelers every Sunday in the fall when I was growing up. For a long time, I harbored dreams of playing ball in the Steel City, but it wasn't meant to be. Doesn't make me any less of a fan, though.

"You can relax. I couldn't care less about the Eagles," Nurse Payne says, typing something into the computer. "I don't even like football."

Nobody's perfect, least of all me.

"That's it." I throw my hands up in mock horror. "We can no longer be friends."

She laughs, her shoulders relaxing for the first time since she entered the room. "I'm your nurse, not your friend."

"Who says you can't be both?" I challenge.

"My clinical instructor, the hospital board of directors, Nurse Rogers." She pauses and arches a slender brow. "There's a reason the hospital has rules against fraternizing with patients."

"I'm going to let you in on a little secret," I stage-whisper. "Rules are meant to be broken."

"Not that rule," she says, crossing her arms over her chest.

"Damn. I never thought my new BFF would be such a rule follower." I grin, giving her what I hope is a charming smile. "You need to live a little."

Her eyes shutter and I realize too late I've said the wrong thing.

"The last time someone told me that, it didn't end well."

"You know what they say. No risk, no reward." I shrug and reach around to fluff up my pillow. "Me? I like to roll the dice every now and again."

She stares pointedly at my leg. "How'd that work out for you last time?"

Damn. Nurse Payne doesn't pull punches.

And I'm here for it.

"Have we met before?" I narrow my eyes to study her features more closely. Creamy skin. High cheekbones. Ski-slope nose. Still, nothing. "I know it sounds cliché, but I feel like we've met before."

She rolls her eyes. "Let me guess, you never forget a pretty face?"

"Well, now that you mention it..."

"I need to get back out on the floor." She adjusts the stethoscope hanging around her neck. "Just push the call button if you need anything."

"So if I get bored and need someone to talk to,"—I hold up the call button—"I can push this and you'll come check on me?"

"It's a call button. Not an escort service," she warns, pointing a finger at me. "Don't push your luck."

"Wouldn't dream of it."

5

HARPER

It's like everybody's got that Friday feeling.

I'm running around like a madwoman, answering call buttons, checking vitals, and generally trying not to lose my mind. After four days in the surgical unit, I thought I was getting the rhythm of the floor, but no.

Hell, it's all I can do to get the med cart right with Nurse Rogers breathing down my neck.

The only positive? I've been able to avoid Chase's room for most of the day. Which is good since he's taken up permanent residence in my brain. Before I walked into his room this morning, I'd have described my guilt as eleven out of ten. Now it's a solid twenty.

So not the time for dramatics.

Or letting Chase Spellman get up in your head.

Right. This isn't school. If I screw up the meds, there are real consequences. Not that Nurse Rogers won't check my work, but giving her reasons to fail me is high on my list of things not to do. Right above partying on Greek Row, cutting loose, and generally falling prey to any more of Bri's bad ideas.

What about your own impulses?

Nope. Not going there. It's the straight and narrow for me from here on out until graduation.

I glance down the hall at Chase's room. The door is half-closed, giving him a modicum of privacy. He hasn't had any visitors today, and he's got to be bored out of his mind. It's a beautiful day, far too nice to be cooped up in a sterile hospital. Alone, nonetheless.

Shit. Maybe I was too hard on him with the whole *don't-abuse-the-call-button* thing. From what I can tell, he's the only patient on the floor who hasn't used it all day.

I bite my lower lip. Maybe I should go check on him? Just to make sure he doesn't need anything.

I drum my fingers on the top of the cart, considering.

It's the least I can do, right?

But no, I've already done enough. How would Chase feel if he knew I was the reason he was laid up in that bed, forced to withdraw for the semester? He'd made it seem like no big deal, but I'm not stupid. Losing scholarship money and withdrawing?

That's a big freaking deal.

He was probably just trying to save face. No one is that forgiving. And having the person responsible nurse you back to health? Talk about kicking a guy while he's down.

"Miss Payne."

"Huh?" I glance up to find Nurse Rogers watching me.

"You better get your head on straight." She plants a hand on her bony hip. "You mess up those meds and you'll never get your license."

Thanks for the reminder.

"Of course." I force a smile. "All set."

She eyes me warily, the look on her face making it clear she finds me lacking in every possible way.

What is her deal? Shouldn't she be like, I don't know?

Encouraging? I don't need to be coddled, but a little less fire and brimstone would be nice.

Maybe she's too jaded to remember her own terrifying nursing clinicals.

An alert sounds and we both look up to see the light flashing above room 1953.

Chase's room.

"Go check on the patient and see what he needs while I look over this," she says, gesturing to the med cart.

My palms start to sweat and I wipe them on my pants as I make my way down the hall.

Don't be such a coward.

I know I'm supposed to look at Chase like any other patient, but from the moment we met, he's put me off-balance. I like to think of myself as a confident woman, comfortable in her own skin, but the truth is, I have insecurities, just like everyone else. And right now I am terrified he will find out I was responsible for his accident.

I tap gently on the door to his room before pushing it open. It's not like I'm going to catch him in a compromising position—the guy can't even get out of bed—but it feels like common courtesy to announce my arrival before busting in.

"What's up?" I ask, forcing a bright smile even as Chase's face falls. His jovial smile disappears so quickly it's possible I imagined it.

Nice to see you too.

Smile frozen in place, I cross the room. My shoes squeak on the tile floor—once, twice, three times—and when I reach his bedside, I reset the call button.

Chase sighs, his broad chest rising and falling beneath the snug hospital gown. "Well, shit. This is embarrassing."

I snort. "Whatever it is, trust me, you aren't the first."

He shoots me a dubious look, but doesn't elaborate.

"In case you haven't noticed, this is a hospital." I gesture to the beige walls and bland tile floor. "It's the one place in the world where there's no room for modesty. I swear, whatever it is, we've seen it before."

Well, Nurse Rogers probably has. Me? Not so much. But I'm working on my bedside manner and I doubt he'd find that little gem comforting.

"Maybe you could get the other nurse?" he suggests, glancing hopefully at the door.

Seriously? I know I'm a student nurse, but he had no problem with me providing care this morning when he was in full-on flirt mode. "How about you tell me the problem and then I can decide if we need reinforcements?"

I have no idea what I'm dealing with here, but I do know that Nurse Rogers will be too happy to mention in her weekly write-up that the patient asked for a different nurse.

"I need to…" He gestures vaguely toward the foot of the bed.

"You need to what?" I ask, perplexed.

He rolls his eyes and rakes a hand through his hair. The blond wave immediately flops back down over his forehead, just as stubborn as its owner. "I, uh, need to take a piss."

My cheeks heat and I curse whatever gene it is that makes me blush at basically everything. I'm a nurse, for crying out loud. I'm not supposed to be embarrassed by bodily functions.

Not even when facing a stone-cold hottie.

"I need a urinal," he explains. "The other nurse forgot to leave it by the bed."

Nursing 101: Never leave a bedridden patient without a bedpan. Or a urinal.

"No problem." I channel my best Nurse Rogers impression and give him a curt nod. "See? That wasn't so hard, was it?"

"You ever had to ask one of your hot classmates for a plastic bottle to pee in?" he asks, lips twisting in a wry grin.

"Nope." I grab the plastic urinal from the bathroom and hand it to him. "But you know what they say. No good deed goes unpunished."

"Good deed?" he asks, a deep groove forming between his brows.

Shit. I so didn't mean to say that.

"The story is all over campus. Not to mention social media." I shrug, feigning indifference. That part is true, at least. Girls all over campus are swooning at the prospect of a modern-day Prince Charming, willing to scale tall buildings and shatter bones to defend their honor and rescue lost sandals. "I think the hashtag was #princecharmingfallshard."

Talk about on the nose.

"In retrospect, probably not my finest moment," he says with a self-deprecating smile.

Tell me about it. There are no winners here. He's got a broken leg and I've got a metric ton of guilt.

Not to mention a single lonely sandal to remind me of the worst night of my life.

6

CHASE

"We all make mistakes," Nurse Payne says, toying with her stethoscope. "Pretty sure it's part of the whole college experience. I'm told the key is not to repeat them."

"I'll be sure to remind my parents of that when they visit this weekend." Not that it'll make a difference with my dad.

She winces. "I take it they're not happy?"

I nod. "They've been pretty cool so far, but now that I'm out of the SICU, I have a feeling I'm in for one of my dad's famous lectures."

He's always been hard on me, determined to make sure I have opportunities he never had growing up. I get it. Life hasn't been easy for him, and he doesn't want to see me struggle the way he and my mom have. I just hope I haven't thrown it all away in one moment of blind stupidity.

"To be fair," she says, eyes glowing fiercely in the afternoon light. "You kind of deserve it. You scared the crap out of m—*them*."

"Trust me." I point at the brace on my leg. "I've learned my lesson. No more dares for me."

I'm done with that shit. If it weren't for my stupid pride, I never would've scaled the drainpipe. I don't remember much about that night—a result of the concussion—but I remember that much, at least. I was so busy trying to prove myself to a couple of drunk assholes that I let myself and my team down. Hell, I could've died.

Talk about screwed-up priorities.

"Probably a good idea." She flashes a brilliant smile. "I think one stay at WUMC is more than enough to fulfill the 'make foolish mistakes' graduation requirement."

"Amen to that." I laugh, a full belly laugh, and the movement causes my leg to shift. Searing pain lances through my left calf and I gasp at the painful reminder of my foolishness.

"Breathe through it." Nurse Payne's voice is a soothing balm as she rests a hand on my shoulder. Her touch is a reassuring weight and when she squeezes gently, I exhale, my whole body relaxing as the discomfort resides. "How would you rate your pain on a scale of one to nine and three-quarters?"

It takes me a minute to get the Harry Potter reference—I blame the concussion—but I smile. "As long as I don't move around too much, it's not so bad. Maybe like a two or three?"

"Let me know if anything changes, okay?" She gives my shoulder another squeeze, her touch lingering before she drops her arm to her side. "No need to suffer unnecessarily just because you're a big strapping football player."

"You think I'm big and strapping?" I wiggle my brows for good measure, which earns me an eye roll.

"You know what I mean," she says with a huff. "Most people aren't used to getting tackled by three-hundred-pound dudes running at full speed."

This time, I roll my eyes. "And you said you weren't interested in football. Sounds like you've got a pretty good handle on the game."

"Doesn't everyone at Waverly?" She widens her eyes. "The student handbook said it was a requirement for admission."

When Nurse Payne first entered my room, I thought it was another stroke of bad luck, but as it turns out, she's far more relaxed without her supervisor peering over her shoulder. I'm all for it. Problem is, my bladder is about three seconds from complete and utter humiliation.

As much as I want her to stay, I need her to go. My mom would kill me for pissing in front of a lady, and if I don't take care of business soon, my bladder's going to explode.

"Hey," I say, an idea taking hold. "Do you think you could get me a popsicle?"

"Yeah." She nods thoughtfully. "I think we have some in the freezer. Any particular flavor?"

"Cherry." I wink at her. "It's my favorite."

And just like that, Nurse Payne is blushing again, her cheeks turning a deep shade of crimson as she backs out of the room.

I quickly take care of business and settle back into my bed, waiting for her return. The clock moves impossibly slow, and while she's only gone five minutes, it feels like an eternity. It's even worse than watching the play clock count down when the game's on the line.

"It must be your lucky day," she says when she finally returns, brandishing the frozen treat like a prize. "You got the last cherry one."

Our fingers brush as she hands it to me and a jolt of awareness shoots up my arm at the skin-to-skin contact. Our eyes meet and once again, I have the feeling we've met before. Or maybe she's just one of those people you feel like you've always known. Whatever the case, there's a connection between us, a pull that defies logic. She must feel it too because she doesn't move her hand away, not immediately anyway.

But then, reality comes crashing in and she steps back, shattering the connection.

I should let her get back to work, but I'm enjoying her company too damn much to let her go. Hell, I don't even know her first name. And as sexy as the whole nurse fantasy is, I actually want to know this girl on a personal level.

"So, are you ever going to tell me your name?" I ask, tearing the Popsicle wrapper open to reveal the bright red prize inside.

"Nurse Payne."

She says it so primly I roll my eyes. "Your real name? It's only fair now that we're friends."

"We're not friends." She huffs out a breath, blowing a strand of dark hair out of her face. "But it's Harper."

"It's nice to meet you, *Harper*," I say, testing it out. Her name rolls off my tongue like second nature. "So, Harper, you must be smart as hell if you're a nurse and a Ravenclaw."

Confusion clouds her eyes, and she tilts her head thoughtfully.

I point to her scrubs—which have a Ravenclaw crest embroidered over her left breast—with my Popsicle.

"Oh, right." She gives herself a facepalm. "Tell it to Nurse Ratched."

I laugh at the reference, which is spot on, but this time I'm careful not to move my leg, even if it might earn me another of Harper's gentle touches.

"Honestly?" She tucks the loose curl back into her ponytail. "I'm starting to completely question all my life choices, including nursing."

Something about the wording tugs at a memory, but it's elusive and I'm not trying to bring on another concussion-induced headache. Not when I've got the undivided attention of a beautiful woman. "Why is that?" I ask, focusing instead on her admission. From what I've seen, Harper is a natural.

"It just feels like no matter how much I study—and trust me, it's a lot—I can't get ahead." She sighs and shoves her hands in her pockets. "All I've ever wanted to do is help people, but I'm not so sure I'm cut out for it."

Is she for real?

"Bullshit. You're taking excellent care of me."

She makes that sassy little snort and I swear to God it's the sexiest thing I've ever heard. A lot of guys on the team enjoy spending time with cleat chasers who just want to worship their bodies, but not me. I'll take a woman who knows her own mind and isn't afraid to showcase it every day of the week. As far as I'm concerned, smart is the new sexy.

I should put that shit on a T-shirt.

"No offense, but getting you a urinal and a popsicle doesn't exactly require a lot of skill." She laughs and shakes her head. "Honestly, a well-trained Labrador could handle it."

Ouch. "I'll try to be a little more demanding moving forward."

Harper's not giving herself nearly enough credit. As much as I want to point it out, she doesn't need a bunch of well-meaning platitudes from me. Besides, if I admit her presence alone has improved my mood tenfold, she'll no doubt point out that a dog could do that too.

"Don't go to any trouble on my account." She flashes me a wicked grin. "Unless, of course, you want to let me practice starting an IV on you?"

I shrug and hold out my arm. "Have at it."

"That's not the usual reaction I get from patients," she says, arching a brow.

"What can I say?" I spread my arms wide. "I'm a Hufflepuff. We're all about dedication, loyalty, and patience. Best house of the four, if you ask me."

She laughs and shakes her head. "Why are you telling me all of this?"

"Because we're getting to know one another. Obviously."

"Obviously," she says, drawing out the word.

The door swings open and the lead nurse looks in, eyes narrowing as they land on Harper. What is her deal? It's like Jekyll and Hyde, the way she interacts with Harper versus me. "Let's go, Miss Payne. You're needed on the floor."

Harper stiffens, the light in her eyes dimming as she dips her chin obediently and says, "Of course."

The lead nurse steps out and Harper gives me a little finger wave. "Duty calls."

She turns on her heel and hurries after her supervisor. Maybe it's my imagination, but I swear her hips have a little more sway than they had this morning. "Harper?"

"Yes?" she asks, turning when she reaches the door.

"You know what they say about Hufflepuffs, right?"

"No, what?"

"If you can't *be* a Hufflepuff," I say, flashing her a cocky grin, "*date* one."

She gives an exasperated eye roll, but the corners of her lips twitch. "The hospital has a no fraternization policy, remember?"

How could I forget? "Just give me a little more time. I'll make a rule breaker out of you yet."

"So not happening," she calls over her shoulder as she slips into the hall.

Challenge accepted.

7

HARPER

Monday is proving no less hectic than Friday, but I'm determined to kick ass today. No second-guessing myself, no letting Nurse Rogers intimidate me, no obsessing over Chase Spellman.

Which would be much easier if Bri wasn't blowing up my phone.

Normally I leave my cell at the nurse's station, but since it was going bananas earlier and one of the LPN's thought it might be an emergency, it's now tucked in the pocket of my shirt, along with a notepad and three pens. On silent.

Unfortunately, I can't unsee the last flurry of messages.

> Bri: How's the star patient today?

> Bri: You should go for it. The guy is legit hot. I'd lick him like *lollipop emoji*

> Bri: Also, he scaled a frat house for you, so there's that...

> Bri: I'll bet he has a big *eggplant emoji*

> Bri: Are you ignoring me or are you getting busy with Prince Charming?

Clearly Bri and I need to have the boundaries talk again. Because she has none and obviously wants me to fail my clinicals.

I spent all day Sunday working on patient care plans while she peppered me with questions about Chase. If I didn't know better, I'd think she was over Adam and on to Chase, but she and Adam went out on Saturday night, so apparently she's just that invested in my love life.

Or lack thereof.

Whatever. Even if I wasn't the sole reason Chase had to withdraw for the semester, I don't have time for a boyfriend. Or a situationship. Or even a hookup. Classes start in two weeks and my already packed schedule is only going to get more frantic with study groups wedged into every free moment of the day.

Go to nursing school, they said. It'll be fun, they said.

Pushing all thoughts of Chase aside, I answer a few patient calls, refilling water pitchers and fielding basic requests the nursing staff are too busy to handle. Nurse Rogers has me practice flushing IVs as she administers new medications and I give silent thanks she doesn't ask me to start one. I know I have to learn it eventually, but the last time I tried, it was a disaster.

To be honest, I kind of want to avoid it as long as possible.

If that makes me a coward, so be it.

"Nurse Payne, I need a fall risk assessment," Nurse Rogers calls out as I pass the desk.

"On it," I say, more than happy to sit my butt down for a few minutes and do paperwork.

I take a seat at the desk and pull up the patient chart, carefully reviewing the patient's history and current medications, before I head down the hall to do a live assessment. Once I've completed the Morse Fall Scale and determined the patient is a moderate risk, I write up a brief care plan. I'm feeling confident as I hand it over to Nurse Rogers, but the high is short-lived.

"We're out of sheets and two of the CNAs called out," she says, barely glancing at the work I've done. "I need you to run down to the laundry and get fresh linens."

So much for impressing her with my killer assessment.

And this is why Mondays take a little more coffee and a lot more mascara.

I trudge down to the laundry and get a cart of fresh linens, chalking the assignment up to paying my dues. After all, better bedsheets than bedpans, right?

I'm waiting for the elevator—just me and my ancient linen cart—when a wheelchair rolls up beside me.

"You know, if you keep avoiding me, I'm going to get a complex."

I slowly turn to find Chase in the wheelchair next to me, looking sexy as sin, the thin fabric of the hospital gown straining over his pecs. There's an older woman—a volunteer—in a navy polo shirt and bright pink lipstick escorting him.

"I have no idea what you're talking about," I retort, willing the elevator to hurry the hell up. Sharing an elevator with Chase is the exact opposite of keeping my distance. And, honestly, we both know his ego is in no danger of developing a complex.

I may not know him well, but any guy who climbs a drainpipe in a short-ass toga isn't hurting for confidence.

"You haven't been by my room once today," he says, carrying on the conversation, like this is the most normal thing in the world. Because apparently it's not awkward at all to have a geriatric volunteer listening to our every word. "Not even to say hello. Ergo, you must be avoiding me."

I snort and roll my eyes. "Ergo?"

He shrugs. "Ravenclaws aren't the only ones who can use big words."

"Not sure 'ergo' qualifies as a big word," I blurt out before I can stop myself. "Why are we even talking about this? It's...absurd."

"Spoken like a true Ravenclaw."

"Whatever." I toss my braid over my shoulder. "I'm surprised Nurse Rogers let you leave the floor."

He grins and looks over his shoulder. "Only because the lovely Rosemary helped me convince her. Truth be told, I think Nurse Rogers has a soft spot for me."

"Of course she does, dear," Rosemary says, patting his shoulder. "How could she not?"

How indeed.

"And you are?" Rosemary looks me over and it takes all my self-control not to smooth down my flyaways under her scrutiny.

Perfect hair is not a requirement for being a capable nurse.

Good thing, because judging by my distorted reflection in the elevator doors, my hair is a hot mess.

"I'm Harper." I extend my hand. "I'm a student nurse in the surgical unit."

Her eyes light up and a smile curves across her bright pink lips, reminding me of my grandma. "So you're Harper." She takes my hand in hers and gives it a firm shake. What Rosemary lacks in stature, she more than makes up for in enthusiasm, her silver curls bouncing with each pump of her hand. "Chase has told me all about you."

"Oh, really?" I give Chase a meaningful look. One I hope conveys a whole lot of *What-the-hell-did-you-tell-her?* and *What-the-hell-were-you-thinking?*

He has a concussion, I remind myself. He can't be held accountable for his actions.

The hell he can't.

And, is it me, or does everyone want me to fail my clinicals? First Bri. Now Chase? I need to nip this in the bud.

Now.

Also, where is the freaking elevator?

"When you stopped visiting, I had to find someone to talk to," Chase says, doing a piss-poor job of feigning disappointment. "Rosemary's an excellent listener, though."

So, what? They became BFFs over the weekend?

Oh my God. I don't even care. Why am I letting him draw me into another ridiculous conversation?

"That's great." Thankfully, the elevator dings and the doors slide open with a quiet hiss. "Enjoy the rest of your walk."

Before I can move my cart an inch, Rosemary's got my arm in a death grip. "I'm feeling a bit tired." She looks up at me with soft brown eyes. "Not as young as I used to be, you know. Could you finish Chase's walk? He shouldn't have to suffer because these old bones need a rest."

I turn to Chase and narrow my eyes. I know a setup when I see one, and this is definitely a setup. Rosemary might look like my favorite grandma, but she's as manipulative as my matchmaking Aunt Jean. Honestly, who'd have thought she had it in her?

"I'll take these linens to the surgical unit. You take Chase up to the roof for a spin around the garden."

She can't be serious. I stare at the pair of them, incredulous.

"Well, what do you say?" Chase asks, grinning like the devil he is.

"I need to get back to the surgical unit. Nurse Rogers is expecting me."

"Pishposh," Rosemary says, waving off my concerns. "I'll let Nurse Rogers know you're caring for a patient. This boy needs some fresh air." She pats Chase on the shoulder again. "It's not good for a strapping young man like Chase to be kept indoors."

Like he's a freaking animal or something.

Here's the thing. Rosemary might weigh a buck ten soaking wet. If she's too tired to push Chase, she's too tired to push my big-ass linen cart.

"I really don't think this is a good—"

Before I can finish, Rosemary moves, quick as a flash. She grabs my cart and pushes it into the elevator. Me? I just stand there and watch, slack-jawed. I mean, it's not like I can wrestle it away from her. What if she falls and breaks a hip?

Besides, as a nursing student with one week of experience, literally everyone outranks me. Including misguided, matchmaking volunteers.

The doors slide shut and I sigh. "I'm totally going to fail my clinicals."

"No way. Nurse Rogers loves me," Chase says, flashing that annoyingly cocky grin of his. "But, hey, if you do fail, you might as well have fun doing it, right?"

8

CHASE

HARPER'S quiet as we wait for another elevator to come. I don't push her. It's obvious she needs a minute to process. Which I get. Rosemary can be a lot to handle, but damn if I don't love that little firecracker.

I should've known she'd pull something like this the moment we saw Harper standing there.

Not that I'm complaining. I've been itching to spend more time with my favorite nurse and she made it happen.

Besides, Rosemary was right. Being cooped up in the hospital sucks. It was the longest weekend of my life, bar none. A few of the guys stopped by to hang on Saturday, and on Sunday, I spent the day in my room watching the Steelers pound the Browns with my parents. But being laid up when the sun's shining outside? It's basically the worst.

I'd rather stare down a fifty-yard field goal with two seconds left on the clock.

When the elevator finally arrives, Harper wheels me in backward, her sweet cherry blossom scent filling the small space. I inhale deeply. She smells like a dream—proving the endless tang of disinfectant hasn't completely deadened my sense of smell—but my enthusiasm comes to a quick end when she pushes the button for the fifth floor.

So much for spending time with my favorite nurse.

"I thought we were going to check out the rooftop garden?" I say, disappointment coursing through my veins.

"We are, but this elevator won't take us all the way up. We need to switch on five."

We get out on the fifth floor, Harper taking care to keep my left leg, which is sticking straight out thanks to a raised leg rest, clear of obstacles.

"Thanks for doing this," I say, as she pushes me down the hall. "I was going stir-crazy back in my room."

"No visitors?" she asks, a note of surprise in her voice.

"Not today. The guys have training camp and my parents are working. They run the local hardware store in Millheim." I adjust my arms on the armrests, trying to get comfortable. These chairs were clearly not made for big guys. "You know how it is. No rest for the weary. It's one of the reasons my parents have pushed me so hard to get a degree," I admit. "I'll be the first college graduate in my family when I get back to campus."

"That's amazing," she says, her voice thick with an emotion I can't identify. "Your parents must be really proud."

"You have no idea." We roll past a nursing station, but no one pays us any attention. It's brighter and more cheerful here than in the surgical unit. Colorful posters and murals line the walls, and if it weren't for Harper, I'd be asking for a transfer. "Our family room is like a shrine to every academic and athletic achievement of my life. My mom is *that* mom. It used to embarrass the hell out of me, but I'm pretty much used to it now."

Harper laughs and there's a levity I haven't heard before. It's nice and if anyone deserves it, she does. From what I've seen, she's a hard worker, busting her ass to finish her degree and dedicating herself to others. "Sounds nice."

"Play your cards right and I'll invite you over to see the plastic trophy I won in the third grade spelling bee." I tilt my head back and when she glances down, I wink at her. "Second place, baby."

She bursts out laughing, quickly slapping a hand over her mouth as we pass a surly looking old dude in a white coat.

"What about your parents?" I ask, determined to untangle the puzzle that is Harper Payne. Despite my attraction to her, I don't actually know much about her. "Do you come from a long line of do-good medical professionals?"

"Not quite," she says, and I can hear the smile in her words. "My parents are both dentists."

"No shit." I sit up straight. "Just like Hermione Granger?"

She laughs and this time it's deep and throaty, the kind of sexy sound that has me imagining other uses for her mouth. "I never would've guessed Waverly's starting kicker was such a Potterhead."

I shrug. "There are worse things to be."

We've nearly reached the end of the hall, and as we roll past a large room with floor-to-ceiling windows, I throw up a hand, signaling for Harper to stop. "Have you been holding out on me, Nurse Payne?"

The wheelchair comes to a stop and I scan the room, which is finished with hardwood floors, colorful furniture that looks way more comfortable than anything in my room, and the pièce de résistance—a media center complete with Xbox.

Harper leans down, lips so close to my ear I can feel the warmth of her breath on my cheek. "It's a teen lounge. Emphasis on teen."

"But they have video games," I argue, raising my arms in protest. "Just let me play one game."

She cocks a brow and gives me a wicked smile. "Sorry, Chase. Can't do it. Hospital rules."

"Again with the rules?" Harper's blue eyes dance with mischief. Hell, maybe she brought me past the lounge just to torture me. "I'll be quick. I promise."

She rolls her eyes and huffs out a laugh. "Words every woman wants to hear."

And with that, we're off again, my chair rolling slowly over the tile floor.

"If I didn't know better," I grumble, "I'd say you're enjoying this."

"Maybe just a little," she admits.

I twist in my chair, careful not to move my leg. "What kind of nurse enjoys seeing her patients suffer?"

She presses her lips flat, but I can tell she's trying to suppress a smile. "You're right. I'm sorry."

"If you want to make it up to me, we can always find a closet and make out."

I'm only half-joking. Because the idea of holding Harper in my arms and kissing those sexy heart-shaped lips of hers? I've been fantasizing about it since the moment she first set foot in my room.

"Yeah, that's definitely not happening," she says, laughing. "Rules, remember?"

Fuckin' rules.

"This place sucks," I mutter, slouching back in my wheelchair. "If I'd known what I was getting myself into, I never would've gone up on that roof."

Not entirely true, because even though I'm starting to think Harper's a masochist—tempting me with video games I can't play is just cruel—I'm glad I had the opportunity to meet her. She's sweet and funny, and I love how she gives as good as she gets. I've never dated a girl like her.

And you never will at this rate.

"Why did you go up on that roof?" she asks, the question slicing through my thoughts as we stop at the rooftop elevator.

Something tells me she's not asking about the shoe or the dare. She already knows that side of the story, thanks to social media. No, there's a deeper meaning to the question, but for the life of me, I'm not sure what she wants me to say. Bringing up Red feels wrong. I'm not about to jeopardize my...whatever Harper and I have...talking about another woman. One who didn't even check to make sure I was okay after the ambulance carted me off. Talk about misreading the room. I actually thought she was into me. And it's almost too simplistic to say that I'm a prideful idiot, though it's the truth.

"Honestly? I'm not even sure I know anymore. The whole night is a blur." I pause, exhaling through my nose as a dull throb pounds against the base of my skull. Maybe this walk wasn't such a good idea after all. I didn't take the doc seriously when he said to take it easy. I'm a D1 athlete, for fuck's sake, but yeah, this whole experience has taken its toll, physically and emotionally. "I know social media's saying I'm some kind of modern-day Prince Charming, but it couldn't be further from the truth. Hell, I didn't even get the girl. Just her shoe."

Harper freezes, her finger halfway to the elevator button. "You still have the shoe?"

"Ironic, right?" I rub the back of my neck and look up at her. "The guys on the team dropped it off Saturday. Put it on a little blue pillow and everything."

"So you're going to try to find her?" she asks, wariness creeping into her voice as she jabs the up button. "The girl from the party, I mean."

And this is exactly why I didn't want to talk about Red with Harper. Whatever interest I had in Red, it's nothing compared to the connection I feel with Harper. I'm not the kind of guy to chase a woman who's not interested any more than I'm the sort to play the field. I need Harper to know that, too.

"You can't seriously think I'm still interested in her after everything that's happened?" I reach up and clasp her wrist, wrapping my fingers around her slender wrist. "There's only one woman I'm interested in getting to know, and she's right here."

Now if I could just convince her to give me a chance.

9
HARPER

BY THE TIME the end of my shift rolls around, I'm tired as hell and my guilt has reached new levels of soul-crushing despair. Chase said it himself. I'm the worst. Well, okay, maybe he didn't use those *exact* words, but his feelings for Red—*for me*—were pretty clear.

Like he said, how could he possibly be interested after everything that's happened?

I don't blame him. I don't. If he knew *I* was Red? He'd never look at me the same way again. Which would be a shame because the idea of making out with Chase in a closet? I've got to admit, the suggestion held some appeal, even if it was inappropriate as hell.

Still, it's my fault he's laid up with a broken leg, cut off from everyone and everything he loves. The least I can do is try to make his stay at WUMC a little easier.

I straighten my spine and square my shoulders, forcing a bright smile as I knock on his door.

There's a muffled reply, which I assume is consent to enter. I push the door open, pulling my cart behind me.

Chase's smile widens when he sees me, and suddenly I don't

have to work quite so hard at my own smile. I don't know how he manages it, but despite the circumstances, he's always upbeat. The energy is infectious.

"Isn't your shift over?"

"Yeah, but I thought you might want some company." I hold up the deli bag. "I come bearing sandwiches."

His eyebrows shoot up and I notice the half-eaten tray of cafeteria food beside his bed. "My hero," he says, making grabby hands. "Seriously, hospital food is the worst. I don't even know what that's supposed to be."

I glance at the congealed lump of...I don't know what, and drop the paper bag on his nightstand. "That's disgusting."

"Tell me about it. Just be glad you don't have to eat it." I avert my eyes as he adjusts his gown, making sure all the important bits are covered. As usual, the blankets are pushed down and his broken leg is propped up on a stack of pillows. The hospital is like a freezer, but the cold doesn't seem to bother Chase. "It tastes even worse than it looks."

Hard to imagine, but I'm willing to take his word for it because no way in hell am I putting that lumpy brown slop in my mouth.

"I got turkey and roast beef," I tell him, pulling two sandwiches wrapped in white paper from the bag. "I wasn't sure what you'd like."

"Anything's better than that." He jerks his chin toward the abandoned tray. "I'll take whatever you don't want."

"So accommodating."

He shrugs, a smile tugging at the corner of his lips. "I try."

I roll my eyes and hand him the roast beef. "Really? I don't remember you being this accommodating when I'm on duty."

He flashes a wicked grin and heat pools low in my belly. "What would be the fun in that?"

Touché.

I pull two Cokes and a package of chips from the bag and set everything up on his bedside tray. I have to give Chase credit. Though he's got to be starving—he's a big dude after all—he waits for me to start. I drag a chair up next to the bed and settle in cross-legged to eat my sandwich.

"Oh, my God," I practically moan. "It feels so good to be off my feet."

"Long day?" he asks, watching me wiggle into a comfy position.

"The longest." And, realizing how that sounds, I hastily add, "But totally worth it. I'm learning a lot."

"Thank you for dinner." He holds up the sandwich. "You didn't have to do all this, and I appreciate it."

Guilt claws at my chest, because no way should he be thanking me for anything. "Just doing my part to nurse Waverly's star kicker back to health."

While also ogling his sculpted pecs like a creeper.

"Duly noted, but your efforts are appreciated, nonetheless." He laughs and shakes his head. "Careful, Harper. You keep talking like that and I'll make a fan out of you yet."

If I'm not careful? That ship has sailed. I may not be a fan of football, but I am a fan of Chase Spellman. Not that I'd ever tell him. Lord knows his ego is big enough. Plus, there's no future, so what's the point?

Still, he *is* nice to look at.

We eat in companionable silence, a sports show playing quietly on the TV as we devour our sandwiches. I missed lunch, thanks to our rooftop foray, but it was worth it to see the smile on Chase's face. The guy hadn't been outside in over a week and it was hard to tell if he was more excited by the fresh air or the sunshine.

Either way, the rooftop circuit was a hit and I've added a recommendation for carefully supervised recreation to his care plan. To keep his spirits up and promote healing. Not because I enjoyed spending time with him.

Liar, liar, pants on fire.

Whatever. Fine. So I enjoy Chase's company. It doesn't mean I'm going to take Bri's advice and suck him like a Blow Pop.

He sighs heavily. "That was amazing."

"Huh?"

Oh, God. Was I thinking out loud?

"The food," Chase says, a wrinkle forming between his brows.

"Right. The food." I ball up my sandwich wrapper and scramble to my feet, cleaning up the remnants of our meal as he turns his attention to the cart by the door.

"What's that?"

"Just a little something I picked up from Pediatrics." I toss the food wrappers into the trash, unable to suppress the grin that splits my face. "I figured you might be up for a little Xbox before I head out."

"Sandwiches and video games?" He winks at me, eyes crinkling at the corners. "You really are the perfect woman."

My cheeks heat and awareness hums across my skin. *If only that were true.* "I wouldn't go that far."

"I would."

Just like that. No qualifiers. No embarrassment. Bold as you please.

You're the one who told him this was no place for modesty.

Taking a page out of his playbook, I add a little swagger to my walk as I push the game cart over to the bed. "You might want to reserve judgment until after I've finished kicking your butt."

"Damn." He rubs his chest, like he's massaging an invisible wound. "So it's like that?"

"What can I say?" I cock a hip and flip my braid over my shoulder. "I'm feeling pretty confident."

"We'll see." He gestures to the game console. "What game are we playing?"

I grab the games and hold them up. "I've got Monopoly and Wheel of Fortune."

He winces. "Monopoly it is. I may be a jock, but I'm not a dumb jock. No way I'm playing a brain game against a Ravenclaw."

"I thought for sure you'd choose Wheel of Fortune." I smirk. "I mean, you did win second place in your spelling bee."

"Yeah, yeah." He rolls his hand, making the universal sign for *get on with it*. "Keep coming with the smack talk. We'll see who lands on top."

Our eyes meet and heat flares white-hot between us. My heart slams against my rib cage, and just when I'm sure he's going to make a dirty joke, he says, "Let's make it interesting."

Warning bells clang in my head, but I ignore them, good sense flying right out the window. Chase tends to have that effect on me. "What did you have in mind?"

"If I win," he says slowly, tongue darting out to lick his lips, "you go on a date with me. If you win, I'll give you a foot massage."

The prospect of a foot massage is practically orgasmic—my arches are screaming for relief even now—but I rally my willpower.

Not gonna lie. I have to dig deep.

"No deal." I scoff and cross my arms over my chest. "It would be incredibly unprofessional to date a patient."

"I won't be your patient forever," he says smoothly, clearly having given this argument some thought. "You know what I think? I think you're just using the whole 'no fraternization' thing as an excuse."

"This isn't nineteen-fifty. I don't need an excuse to turn down a date."

"Oh, I know." He grins, the corner of his mouth edging toward a smirk. "But as long as you're throwing out excuses, you don't have to face the truth."

"Which is what?" I ask, fear creeping up my spine. He can't know the truth. There's no way. If he did, he wouldn't be smiling. He'd be tossing me out on my ass.

"You're afraid to let your guard down around me."

Relief washes over me. My secret is safe—*for now.*

"We have chemistry, Harper. The scorching-hot kind," he says, lifting a brow. He's not wrong, but it'll take a hell of a lot more than sizzling chemistry to make this work. Like, a total rewrite. "You can ignore it, but that won't change the fact that it's there, simmering just below the surface."

Stay strong, girl.

Easier said than done when he's looking at me like a triple hot fudge sundae with a cherry on top.

"Whatever." I pop the disc into the game console and toss him a controller. "Are you ready to do this or what?"

He catches the controller easily, which I guess is no surprise, because...*football player.*

"I'm not the one afraid to make the wager." He chuckles. "So much for all that talk of kicking my ass. I thought you were tougher than this, Payne."

I finish setting up the game, refusing to be baited.

"Man, it must suck knowing you've lost before the game even starts," he says, in what has to be the most patronizing voice I've heard in all my life. "I've never even lost a game of Monopoly."

I give him a saccharine smile and take my seat, tucking my legs beneath me. "Well, there's a first time for everything. I'll be sure to take a picture of your sad face so your mom can add it to the Chase Spellman shrine."

"Damn. Did you just make a mom joke?" He pretends to dust off his shoulder. "Now I know you're scared."

"Of losing at Monopoly?" I arch a brow. "I can assure you my ego isn't that fragile." I stare pointedly at him. "Unlike some people."

"I'm not talking about the game. I'm talking about your feelings for me," he says with a self-satisfied smirk. And, oh, do I want to wipe that look off his face. "That's why you won't take the bet, right?"

"You know what? You're on." I jab a finger toward at him. "I'll take your stupid bet, because you're going down."

Unfortunately, my declaration doesn't have the desired effect. In fact, his smile is so freaking wide now he looks like the Cheshire cat.

Probably because I just walked right into his trap.

Now I definitely have to win the game, because if I don't? I'm going on a date with Chase Spellman. And that would be a disaster.

10

CHASE

"Boom!" Harper yells, cheeks flushed, eyes bright as she slaps her controller against her thigh. "Take that, Spellman!"

I can't believe it. She actually beat me. I mean, it's kind of a game of chance, but I was so sure I had it in the bag. Right up until my dumb ass landed on Park Place and went bankrupt.

Harper shoots me a smug grin and pretends to buff her nails on her scrubs. Joke's on her, though, because I'm going to give her a foot rub she'll never forget. By the time I'm done, the hospital's fraternization policy will be the last thing on her mind.

"You wanna do a victory lap or are you ready to come over here and claim your prize?" I ask, pitching my voice low.

She squeaks and hops to her feet, eyes wide. "I'm—I'm going to have to take a rain check."

"No way." I crook a finger toward myself, gesturing for her to come closer. "That wasn't our deal, Harper."

"Technically," she says, toying with the end of her braid, "we never specified a timeline for prize distribution, so..."

"Get your sexy ass over here and let me massage your feet.

You've been taking care of me all day. Now it's my turn to take care of you."

"As lovely as that sounds, that's not really how the whole nurse-patient relationship works."

"You're off duty." I roll my eyes, because damn, what I wouldn't give to be able to get out of this bed. The woman has me at a serious disadvantage and she knows it, keeping just out of my reach. "Besides, I'm going to be released in a few days anyway."

"And yet,"—she gestures to my bed with a broad sweep of her arm—"here you are."

"I'm barely even a patient," I argue, scrambling to make my case. "The doc is just keeping me out of an abundance of caution. I'm sure it's documented on my chart."

"Oh, okay." Sarcasm drips from her words as she packs up the game cart. "I'll be sure to tell that to Nurse Rogers when she fails my ass."

"Now you're just being dramatic," I say, knowing it'll get a rise out of her.

"Says the guy who climbed a drainpipe in a freaking toga."

I ignore that bit. No good will come from talking about that night. Not if Harper still thinks I'm hung up on Red. And while I can see why she might be apprehensive about my intentions, I'm not the kind of guy to fuck around. I don't do casual sex. Hell, I haven't even dated since last year. "Come on. You know you want it."

She turns and shoots me a dark look. "You know you sound like a creeper, right?"

I consider my word choice. "Fair point, but that doesn't make it any less true."

"It's unprofessional."

"It's a foot rub, not a full-body massage," I fire back. "Unless you want to upgrade?"

She rolls her eyes and pushes the cart over to the door. "Hard pass."

Her scrubs are wrinkled and her hair's come loose from her braid. It's been a long day, and she's spent most of it on her feet, so, while there's definitely a part of me that's physically attracted to Harper and would love to get naked with her, that's not what this is about. I just want to do something nice for her, and since I'm stuck in bed, my options are severely limited.

"You've been on your feet all day," I say, trying a different approach. "They have to be killing you. Why not let me massage them?" I hold up my palms. "Strictly platonic. I won't even hit on you."

She snorts. "You say that like it's a sacrifice."

"Trust me, it is."

But it's one I'm willing to make if it puts her at ease, because I'm not just in this for the night, I'm in it for the long haul. I meant it earlier when I said we have chemistry. And I fully intend to explore it, if she'll just give me a chance.

Harper chews her bottom lip, the pink flesh plumping around her teeth. "No funny business?"

"No funny business," I promise, scooting over and patting the empty spot on the bed next to me.

She slides back into the bedside chair and kicks off her Crocs. She hesitates, but then props her feet up on the edge of the bed where I can reach them. I shift, taking in the blue and gold District 12 socks.

"The Hunger Games?" I cup her right heel and gently lift her foot. "You really are a book nerd."

She grins and it lights up her whole her face. "Was there ever any doubt?"

"No, I suppose not." It's on the tip of my tongue to tell her I like smart women, but then I remember my promise not to hit on her, so I'll save that for later.

Though she's quiet as I plant my thumb on the soft underside of her foot and press it into her arch, I'm pretty sure her eyes roll back in her head.

"How's that feel?" I ask, repeating the motion.

"So good I'm trying to remember why this is a bad idea." Her eyes drift shut and she tips her head back, leaning against the chair's headrest.

"I think you mean why it's a good idea." I move on to the ball of her foot, squeezing firmly and moving my thumb in a circular motion.

"You're actually pretty good at this whole foot massage thing," she says, one eye popping open. "If football doesn't work out, you totally have a future as a masseuse."

"Thanks, I think?" I chuckle, sweeping my thumb across her heel, the way the team trainers do after a hard workout. "Pro ball was never my goal. I'm a Communications major. I want to break into sports broadcasting."

"Football?"

"If I'm lucky. The NFL's probably a long shot, but I'd be just as happy with collegiate sports."

Just need to finish my degree first.

My chest tightens and I glance at my left leg. I haven't seen what it looks like underneath all those bandages yet. I close my eyes or stare at the ceiling when the doc comes in to look at it, because, honestly? I'm not sure I could handle the sight.

Not when my whole future is riding on a full recovery.

"You've got a nice voice for broadcast." Harper opens her mouth to say something else, but whatever she's going to say is lost to a quiet moan when I slide my thumb down the arch of her foot. *"Oh-my-God-that-feels-amazing."*

Eager to please, I repeat the motion, earning another breathy moan.

"This is—" She slides down in the chair, arms dangling loosely over the armrests. "So. Relaxing."

"If you like this, I can think of a few other ways to help you relax."

More than a few, actually. And I'd be happy to show her all of them. But that might count as flirting...

"Keep it in your pants, Spellman. Need I remind you the whole reason you're in this hospital is because you were following your penis every which way it waggled?"

Burn.

"First of all, my cock doesn't waggle," I inform her indignantly. "What does that even mean?"

She gives a vague hand gesture and now I'm seriously questioning where she's getting her information. I hope this isn't what they're teaching in nursing school now.

"Yeah. Cocks don't do that," I say, switching feet. "Have you even considered the possibility that my accident was fate's way of bringing us together?"

She laughs. "Not even once, so whatever Florence Nightingale fantasy you've got going on up there," she says, pointing to my head. "It's not going to happen."

"You know Florence Nightingale was chaste, right?"

"Really?" She lifts her head, and I'm pretty sure she's trying to decide if I'm fucking with her again. "How do you even know that?"

"I took a feminism class freshman year," I tell her, flexing her toes with the heel of my palm.

"Let me guess. Easy A?"

"Hell, no. That class was hard as fuck." No lie. It was the hardest class I took freshman year. Granted, it's possible that's because I was basically a caveman, but I like to think I've grown since then. "Nearly killed my GPA, but it was worth it. The class made me think differently, you know?"

She studies me and just when I think I'm starting to win her over, she says, "Whatever. I'm not going to be seduced by a feminist jock, even if it is the hottest thing I've ever seen."

"Never say never," I tease, moving on to her Achilles tendon, which is tight as hell.

"I hate to break it to you," she says, slinging an arm across her forehead. "Your leg is fractured in three places. You can't even go to the bathroom by yourself. You're in no shape to have sex." She lifts her arm and gives me a pointed stare. "Not good sex, anyway."

I promised no flirting, but technically she's the one who brought up sex, so...

"My mouth and fingers work just fine." I sweep my thumb across the arch of her foot to prove my point. "Climb on up here and I'll show you."

Her breath catches and I watch, transfixed, as her chest rises and falls. Her eyes darken and for an instant—just one brief second—I think she's considering it.

"Thanks for the foot massage, but that's as far as this goes." She pulls her feet back and slips them into her Crocs. "Like I said, the last time I cut loose, it didn't end well. It's the straight and narrow for me from here on out."

More like the straight and boring. What is it that has her so shook?

"Do you want to talk about it?" I ask, curiosity piqued. "I'm a pretty good listener."

And not just because I'm bedridden.

"No, thanks." She stands, smoothing the front of her scrubs. "I should get going. I need to return the game cart, and it's getting late."

By AARP standards, yes. For two college students, not so much.

But there's no point pressing the issue. If Harper doesn't

want to talk about it, she won't. She's stubborn as hell and while I admire her for it, it also makes getting to know her...challenging.

"You know where to find me if you change your mind," I say, watching her retreat.

When she reaches the door, Harper looks back over her shoulder. There's a sadness in her eyes that wasn't there before. "I won't."

Déjà vu sweeps over me. I don't know why, but this whole scene feels familiar. Like we've said these words before. But try as I might, the memory slips through my fingers, and I can't shake the feeling I'm doomed to repeat some egregious mistake.

11

HARPER

I SHOULD'VE KNOWN it was going to be a day when I woke to find the sky gray and overcast, but it took a pothole and about four ounces of scalding hot coffee in my lap to drive the point home. Fortunately, the coffee stain mostly blends in with my navy scrubs, so I'm rolling with it. Lesson learned.

Even nursing students should keep a clean set of scrubs handy.

I make a mental note to throw an extra pair in the car as I make the rounds with Nurse Rogers, checking vitals and pushing meds. She's quiet this morning, and I'm calling it a win because at least she's not critiquing my every move.

When we get to Chase's room, he's awake and watching SportsCenter, his leg propped up on a stack of sad-looking pillows. Something's off and it takes me a minute to realize he's wearing real clothes. His faded hospital gown has been replaced by navy athletic shorts and a white tank top.

The better to show off his muscles.

Chase's sculpted pecs are on full display, the thin material of the tank leaving little to the imagination. He's got a deep tan that hasn't yet started to fade, and there's a smattering of gold hair on his chest that's just a few shades lighter than the dirty blond curls on his head. My throat is suddenly parched. It's all I can do not to pour myself a glass of water from the pitcher on the nightstand.

My gaze travels down the ropy muscles of his biceps and lingers on his large, capable hands. Hands that were on my body last night. Sure, he only touched my feet, but technically? Still my body.

Pressure coils low in my belly and— *Nope*. Not going there.

Chase chuckles and I shake off my reverie. I am a professional, after all. And it's not like I've never seen a male chest before.

"Good morning, ladies."

"Morning." I pull up his chart on the computer. "I see you've upgraded from your hospital gown."

"It took a little convincing, but I finally wore the doc down," he says, ruffling a hand through his hair. "And I gotta tell you, I feel a thousand times better. Who knew putting on real clothes could be such a game changer?"

Literally everyone who's ever had to bare their ass in a hospital gown.

That's what I want to say, but I don't, because...Nurse Rogers. She stands beside me, looking over my shoulder as I scan the most recent updates to Chase's file. It's almost a relief when I step away to take his vitals.

The woman gives the phrase *breathing down my neck* new meaning.

"I'm glad you're feeling better today." I move to the sink to wash my hands. *That's it. Just keep it professional.* And hope like hell Chase doesn't bring up last night's foot massage.

"Me too." He flashes me a devilish grin as I grab a paper towel and dry my hands. "What about you? You're looking rather *relaxed* today."

So much for that. I'm starting to think the guy doesn't have a subtle bone in his body.

"How's your pain this morning?" I ask, ignoring his question. No need to encourage him, especially with Nurse Rogers scrutinizing my every move. He shifts slightly when I approach the bed, and though I'm sure he thinks he's doing a great job of hiding his discomfort, I don't miss the way his lips tighten when he moves.

"Nothing I can't handle."

I nod, but say nothing, giving him a chance to elaborate. The doctor scaled back the dose on his painkillers, which means we'll need to keep an eye on his pain level. Something tells me Chase will suffer in silence before admitting there's anything he can't handle.

"Your pillows are looking a little flat." I gesture to the thin stack under his leg.

"It's this damn brace." He glares at the metal contraption, and I can't really blame him because it looks hella uncomfortable. "The weight just crushes the pillows every time I fluff them up."

I turn to Nurse Rogers. "Can we try a few blankets?"

She nods in agreement and a few minutes later, I'm carefully tucking folded blankets under Chase's leg as he watches me work. His left leg is heavily bandaged below the knee, but repositioning him requires that I elevate the entire leg. That means I also have to touch his upper thigh, and every time my fingers dig into the taut muscles, I can't help but remember the Sig party when he told me his legs were his best asset.

He's not wrong. His thighs are thick and well-defined, and it doesn't take a whole lot of imagination to picture myself wedged between them.

Which I definitely should *not* be thinking about right now. Heat floods my cheeks, and I give silent thanks he's wearing shorts and not a hospital gown. The last thing I need is actual images of Chase's cock to keep me up at night.

The guy is already taking up far too much real estate in my brain.

"How's that?" I step back to take a look at my work, making sure his lower leg is fully stabilized.

"Much better." Chase doesn't even look at his leg. His attention is riveted on me, and for one hot minute, I'm convinced he knows all my dirty thoughts.

Hell, I'm convinced he shares them.

"Vitals, Miss Payne." Nurse Rogers makes an impatient noise in the back of her throat. "We don't have all day."

Yes, Nurse Buzzkill.

I fly through Chase's vitals, refill his water pitcher, and before I know it, we're moving on to the next patient.

The rest of the day passes in a blur. We're shorthanded—again—and I haven't had a chance to check on Chase all afternoon. He's been unusually quiet today, so when there's finally a lull in patient calls and Nurse Rogers takes a break, I head down to his room.

I find him playing on his phone, the TV set to a rerun of *The Big Bang Theory*. I love this show, and I can't say I'm surprised Chase is a fan too. Just another thing we have in common, I guess.

He looks up and smiles when he sees me, but it doesn't quite reach his eyes. "Hey."

"Hey, yourself." I study the shadows under his eyes and the tension lines around his mouth. He's been in the hospital for a week and half—which would take a toll on anyone—but something's not right. Just this morning, he was in high spirits. "You've been awfully quiet today. I wanted to make sure you weren't down here getting into trouble before I head out for the day."

Chase gives me his best *Who me?* expression, but says nothing.

That's when I realize his IV is missing.

I pull up his chart on the computer and quickly review the latest notes. He should still be getting painkillers, so...where's the IV?

Suspicion creeps in and I turn to Chase, who's still watching me, lips pressed flat. "What happened to your IV?"

He shrugs, like a disappearing IV is one of life's great mysteries.

I move around the side of the bed and then I see it, lying in a tangled mess next to him.

That is so not okay.

I plant a hand on my hip and point to the discarded IV. "Explain."

"It fell out."

"Yeah, I'm going to call bullshit, because IVs don't just *fall out*," I say, making air quotes.

Not if they're done properly, anyway.

"That one did." He freaking shrugs again and I swear if he does that one more time...

"Chase." My stupid voice wavers, because what the hell was he thinking? This is a surefire way to get himself another infection. And honestly, why would he cut himself off from his pain medication when he so obviously needs it? This whole thing is crazy-pants bananas. "You can't just take out your IV whenever you feel like it."

"Really?" He makes a show of glancing down at his IV-free arm. "Because I just did."

I throw my hands up in disbelief. On the one hand, yay for telling the truth. On the other, WTF? "You know Nurse Rogers is going to make me replace it, right?"

"I do."

"Then why—" *Holy. Crap.* He did this for me. Because I said I needed the practice. My stupid heart melts faster than a single-scoop of mint chocolate chip in July. No one volunteers for an IV stick. No one in their right mind, anyway. "I can't believe you did this," I whisper. "For me."

"You said you needed the practice," he returns, meeting my eye. "Besides, compared to a busted leg, what's one little needle?"

I mean, he's not wrong, but it's too much. If he knew the truth...

"You shouldn't have—"

"You're worth it, Harper Payne." Chase reaches out and takes my hand, his fingers curling possessively around mine. It's totally inappropriate, but for once, I don't fight it. His grip is firm, his touch warm. Everything about it feels right, and I know beyond a shadow of a doubt that he's going to make some woman very happy one day.

And as much as the realization hurts, it won't be me.

12

CHASE

By the time Harper returns with Nurse Rogers and a plastic bin full of supplies, my leg is throbbing. At this point, I'd let her stick me a dozen times if it was the price of relief, because cutting off my painkillers? Not the smartest move.

Still, I don't regret it. Not if it helps Harper.

She may think I'm nuts for removing my IV, but it was time to make a big move. The doc said I'll be released by the end of the week and so far, Harper's resisted all my efforts to woo her.

The fuck? Who even says woo?

Great. I'm delirious with pain.

The point is, I'm running out of time. In a few days, I'll be headed back to Millheim—without Harper's number.

Unacceptable.

I need to convince Harper this connection is worth exploring. But first, painkillers.

Nurse Rogers gives me the side-eye as Harper lays out her supplies, unpackaging tubes and all kinds of weird-looking shit I know is about to be inserted into my body. I should be used to it by now, but nope, all that crap still freaks me out.

"So the IV just fell out?" Nurse Rogers asks, skepticism lining her eyes.

"Yeah, it was the strangest thing." Might as well play the dumb jock card, because I can't exactly tell her this harebrained scheme is a desperate attempt to win Harper over. The fact is, I'm crazy about her, and I'll do whatever it takes to convince her to give me a shot. "I stretched my arms like this," I say, lifting my arms over my head, "and *poof!* It just fell out."

Next to me, Harper snort-laughs before breaking into an unconvincing cough, which results in Nurse Payne ordering her to wash her hands again.

When she returns to the bed, her mouth is set in a grim line. She puts on a clean pair of gloves and opens a sterile wipe to clean the site of my last IV, which is admittedly a bit grisly looking from my hack job. She quickly bandages my inner elbow and begins tapping my forearm, looking for a vein.

"I'm going to try to avoid putting the IV in your hand," she says, not looking up, "but if it falls out again, the hand it is."

"Duly noted." She doesn't state it explicitly, but I'm pretty sure that's supposed to be a warning. Like, don't act up or I'm going to stick this mobility limiting torture device in your hand so I can kick your ass at Xbox again. "But you might want to put a little extra tape on it, just in case."

I don't actually want extra tape—that shit hurts when you rip it off and I'm not trying to have a bald patch on my arm—but my comment has the desired effect. She looks up, the corners of her lips twitching.

Then she turns to Nurse Payne and they have a brief discussion about catheters and cannulas. The technical talk goes over my head, but I don't miss the way Harper's hands shake as she opens the package with the needle and sets it to the side, next to a plunger of saline. That much, at least, I remember from my last IV insertion.

Holding Harper

That shit felt like ice water in my veins.

"All right." Harper flashes me a wobbly smile. It sucks there's not more I can do to put her at ease, because Nurse Rogers and her scowl aren't exactly encouraging. "Just try to relax, Chase. I'm going to apply a tourniquet and clean the skin around the vein. Once it dries, we'll get that IV taken care of, okay?"

"No worries." I want to reach out and touch her, to squeeze her hand and comfort her, but since it would probably be a violation of the fraternization policy, I settle for the three words I know she needs to hear most. "I trust you."

Harper gives a curt nod, eyes brimming with gratitude. Then she expertly ties the tourniquet around my arm, miraculously managing not to pull any hair, which, as far as I'm concerned, is a win. Her touch is featherlight as she swabs my skin and fans it dry with her gloved hand. She picks up the needle, which is smaller than I remember, and her hands are surprisingly steady.

She can do this, I know it. In the short time I've known Harper, I've seen how hard she works, how determined she is to succeed, how much she cares—even when she pretends not to.

Now she just needs to believe it.

I keep my gaze locked on her face as she works. I may have volunteered for this little exercise, but that doesn't mean I plan to watch. She bites her lower lip and there's a small pinch when she inserts the needle. It's nothing compared to the throbbing in my leg, which is becoming more insistent, the sharp jolts of pain pounding in concert with my heart.

I harden my jaw instinctively. Just need to grit it out a little longer. Good practice, I guess, because the doc's already warned me PT and recovery aren't going to be easy.

"That wasn't so bad," I announce, letting my head fall back against the pillows, ready for the juice to start pumping through my IV. "Nice work, Nurse Payne."

"That was the local anesthetic," Harper says apologetically, disposing of the needle in a little red box with a biohazard label. "To numb the site."

Oh, well, then.

"We're almost done," she adds, giving me an encouraging smile. "You'll be pain free before you know it."

I lift my head, prepared to deny it, but Harper's focused on her work and I don't want to interrupt. Better to let her concentrate as she builds her confidence.

How the hell did she know my leg is killing me anyway?

Because you're a piss-poor actor. Obviously.

I hear Harper's sassy tone in that last bit, and I'm grinning like a fool when I feel the pressure of the IV piercing my skin.

"Backflow?" Nurse Rogers asks.

"Got it," Harper answers, clear and confident.

"Make sure you advance the catheter before you withdraw the needle."

Harper nods, a wide grin lighting up her entire face.

"And be sure you tape it down good," Nurse Rogers adds, holding up a wide strip of tape. "We wouldn't want it *falling out* again."

No, we definitely wouldn't want that.

Before I know it, I'm taped up, hooked up, and my pain meds are dripping down the plastic tube at my bedside.

Sweet relief.

Pride shines in Harper's eyes as she cleans up and disposes of the trash. I can't tear my eyes away from her. She's incredible, really. Smart, beautiful, independent. And she's got a heart the size of Wildcat Stadium.

"Nice work," Nurse Rogers trills. The woman is sparing with her words, but for once, it's actually a good thing.

Harper and I both gape at Nurse Rogers. I can't speak for Harper, but it's the first time I've ever heard the lead nurse give her a compliment. I'm so freaking proud of her. I want to leap out of bed and tackle hug her, but, again, *fraternization policy.*

Plus, there's the whole *no putting weight on my leg for eight weeks* thing.

"Agreed," I chime in, winking at Harper. "Easiest IV I've ever gotten."

She flushes a deep crimson and tosses her gloves into the trash. "I'm glad to hear it. Let's just hope it's also the last one you get for a while, shall we?"

"Amen to that." If I never see the inside of a hospital again, I'll die a happy man. "No more rooftops for me. In fact, I'm thinking about trying out this new thing where I stay on the straight and narrow."

"Oh, really?" Harper crosses her arms over her chest, entirely unconvinced.

"Sure," I reply, doing my best to sound innocent when we both know I'm anything but. "Who knows? It could be fun."

She checks to make sure Nurse Rogers isn't looking and rolls her eyes. "Let me know how that works out."

I perk up at this, because, *opening*. "I didn't realize the hospital had a follow-up care program. Will you be keeping in touch once I'm released, Nurse Payne?"

Harper blinks slowly and her eyes slide to Nurse Rogers, like she can't believe I would ask such a thing. In front of her supervisor, nonetheless.

"No, we do not have a *follow-up care* program," she says, placing way too much emphasis on the words. It's pretty obvious what she really means is *I will not be keeping in touch*. Clearly my work here is not done, but I'd be lying if I said I didn't love getting her fired up. She's so cute when she's sassy. "But I'm sure your doctor will match you with a great physical therapist to get you back on your feet."

"Now that you mention it," I say, rubbing the back of my neck, "I'm pretty sure I've met my match."

Harper's mouth falls open and it seems I've rendered her speechless, because no sound comes out, though her cheeks are a lovely shade of pink.

Nurse Rogers opens the door and I swear to God she actually taps her foot as she waits for Harper to join her.

"Will you be here tomorrow? To check on my IV?" I ask, pointing to her handiwork.

"Yes, Chase. Nurse Rogers and I are both on duty tomorrow." She follows the lead nurse into the hall, calling over her shoulder, "Try to stay out of trouble until then, okay?"

13

HARPER

THANKS TO A SCHEDULING MIX-UP, I've been off for the last two days. Which, if I'm being honest, felt like an eternity. Sure, I got a lot of studying done, and even managed to pick up all my books and supplies for fall semester, which was nice, but the guilt's been gnawing at me relentlessly.

And not just because Chase is probably bored out of his mind.

What he did with the IV? That was...completely unexpected. Insane, but unexpected. Over the last week, he's shown me a side of himself I couldn't have imagined existed. No, that's not entirely true. I knew from the moment we met at the Sig party that he wasn't like the other guys I've dated. After all, none of them appreciated my confidence.

But it's more than that.

He's funny. Patient. Loyal. And, let's be honest, the guy does *not* give up.

A Hufflepuff through and through.

Whoever said Hufflepuff was the worst house was a bleeding idiot.

I'm smiling as I step out of the elevator and onto the surgical unit, a plastic tub of chocolate chip cookies resting against my hip. I nearly caved and visited Chase yesterday. I drove to the hospital, fully prepared to hijack a game cart so we could have an epic Xbox rematch, but once I was parked in the lot, I changed my mind.

No matter how much Chase flirts, or how many times I've imagined kissing him, there's no future. Not when the truth of my involvement in his injury—in ruining his life—would destroy whatever it is that's going on between us. I've turned it over in my mind a thousand times and no matter how you spin it, the end result is the same.

Which is depressing as hell. Ergo, cookies.

Because when you're stressed, what could be better than fresh-from-the-oven chocolate chip cookies? Nothing, that's what. I ate nearly a dozen of them myself before packing up the rest to share with Chase and the nursing staff.

And, okay, yes, I ate one for breakfast too, because...no self-control.

I step off the elevator, confirming my shift doesn't start for another ten minutes. Just enough time to pop into Chase's room and drop off some cookies. My shoes squeak as I make my way down the hall, but the unit looks the same as always—bright, white, sterile.

When I reach Chase's room, the door is partially open, but the light is off and, for an instant, I wonder if he's still sleeping. I can't remember a morning where he wasn't up watching cartoons, but there's a first time for everything, so I ease the door open slowly.

If he's asleep, I don't want to wake him. It's hard enough to get a decent night's rest in the hospital with the nursing staff constantly checking IVs and vitals.

I'll just peek in and—

The room is empty. Not *the-patient's-in-Radiology-empty*, but *empty-empty*. The bed has been stripped and there's not a single card or personal item to be found. My fingers itch to check the nightstand drawer for any sign of Chase—lip balm, his wallet, the stupid freaking sandal that started this whole mess—but my feet are rooted to the ground.

Chase is gone.

"The doctor released him early," one of the CNAs says, breezing past with an armload of sheets. "You just missed him."

My stomach drops and there's a bitter taste in my mouth that has nothing to do with the half cup of coffee I managed to guzzle on the drive over. Coffee that's now a lead weight in my belly.

So that's it. Chase is gone. I didn't even get to say goodbye.

Disappointment grips my chest like a vise, squeezing the air from my lungs.

I knew this was coming, knew he only had a few more days until release, but not once did it occur to me that he might not be here today. While I spent the last two days shopping for books and baking cookies, he was preparing to go home. Probably learning to maneuver his own wheelchair and get around on crutches.

Should've put on your big-girl pants and visited when you had the chance.

Chase will be heading back to Millheim with his family to recover, and since he's withdrawn from school, I'll have no way to contact him.

Dammit. How long does the university even wait to shut off your email when you withdraw? Or maybe he's on social media?

Yeah, because stalking former patients wouldn't be inappropriate—*at all*.

I don't want to lose Chase. Not now. Not like this.

The realization hits me right in the feels, so sharp and so clear I don't know how I missed it before.

Because you're a hardhead.

I turn on my heel and sprint for the elevator, cookie tub clutched to my chest. The CNA said I just missed him. Maybe it's not too late. Maybe I can still catch him. Discharges require paperwork and paperwork takes forever, right?

I skid to a stop at the elevator and jab the down button. The light comes on, but the elevator moves at a snail's pace, and the floor designator seems to be stuck on two. Heaving a frustrated sigh, I give up on the elevator and take the stairs, racing down them at a breakneck speed, my feet on autopilot.

At least if I break my neck, I'm in the right place.

The stairwell is empty and when I reach the ground floor, I leap over the last two steps and fling the door open, making a beeline for the main lobby. My heart's pounding and my breath comes hard and fast as I enter the atrium. It's quiet. Just the usual hum of the hospital waking up for the day with bodies coming and going, muted news stations, and somewhere close by, a vacuum that sounds like it's on its last leg.

I scan the waiting area, but there's no sign of Chase, only a middle-aged couple whispering in hushed tones.

Am I too late?

More like too stubborn.

The glass doors at the lobby entrance slide open and an elderly volunteer pushing an empty wheelchair enters.

Hope surges, fizzing in my chest like one of those overpriced bath bombs Bri loves.

I force myself to walk slowly—okay, maybe not slowly, but at a pace that won't incite panic—toward the doors. They open with a quiet *whoosh* and I step out into the humid August air. In about three seconds, the rebellious curls around my face will be fighting their way free of my ponytail, but for once, I don't mind.

After all, I'm a woman on a mission.

Operation: Get the guy.

I scan the parking lot, using my hand to shield my eyes. The sun is shining and there's an ambulance pulling around to the Emergency Room on the west side of the hospital, but still no Chase.

And all that hope fizzing in my chest? Flatter than a day-old soda.

My shoulders sag and I nearly drop the cookie tub as disappointment sets in.

I'm too late. I blew it. I had one chance to make things right, and instead, I took the coward's way out, too worried about rules and repercussions to roll the dice. Maybe Chase was right. Maybe it wasn't karma that brought him back into my life, but fate.

Not that it matters now.

I turn to re-enter the hospital and that's when I see him. Chase. He's sitting on a metal bench with a small duffel bag, his left leg stretched out in front of him and a pair of crutches leaning against the stone pillar beside him. He's clean-shaven, square jaw on full display, and for once, his hair is pushed back from his face, giving an unobstructed view of those icy blue eyes. The Waverly Wildcats T-shirt he's wearing is stretched taut across the muscles of his chest, which I'll admit is nice, but it's his brilliant smile that nearly does me in.

Hell, my knees buckle when he turns the full force of that perfect smile on me.

I'm not too late.

"Chase."

"Harper," he says, mimicking me playfully. "Come to say goodbye?"

I nod, scrambling for words. I acted on impulse coming down here. I didn't have time to consider what I'd say if I found Chase, and now that he's right here in front of me, I'm at a loss.

After all, how do you even begin to apologize for destroying someone's life?

And I need to apologize.

Because finding Chase's room empty this morning? The crushing disappointment that swept over me? It made me realize the value of our connection. A connection we've barely even begun to explore. I'm swamped with school and study groups and clinicals, but I know, deep in my gut, that if I don't do this, I'll regret it.

Maybe for the rest of my life.

So, yeah. I have to come clean and face the consequences, even if it means Chase hates me for what I've done. As terrifying as the prospect is, it's the right thing to do. I don't want to carry this guilt anymore, and although he may never want to see me again, we can't move forward without honesty.

I can either walk away now or take the leap and maybe —*with a little help from the universe*—get the guy.

14

CHASE

I CAN'T BELIEVE Harper's really here. After two days without contact, I'd nearly resigned myself to the idea that she was avoiding me. I'd hoped she would show, but I guess deep down I hadn't believed it.

Not after she'd missed two shifts in a row.

She watches me, clutching a plastic container to her chest and chewing her bottom lip.

Well, this is awkward.

"My dad is pulling the car around," I explain, raking a hand through my hair as I search for words.

Who needs words? Just ask for her number already.

"So, I was thinking—"

"I'm glad I caught you," Harper says, cutting me off as the words come tumbling out rapid-fire. "I was afraid you'd already be gone. I made you cookies," she adds, stepping forward and thrusting a plastic container at me.

"Cookies, huh?" I grin up at her and take the tub, sitting it on the bench next to me. "What about the no-fraternization rule?"

Because, yeah, I'm an idiot.

"I wanted to talk to you about that, actually." She tucks a

loose curl behind her ear as she lowers herself onto the bench next to me. Then she pulls a pair of tiny scissors from her pocket, grabs my wrist, and snips off my hospital wristband. She smiles broadly, her face just inches from mine. This is the closest we've been, sitting shoulder to shoulder, hip to hip, our mouths a breath apart. "You are officially no longer a patient."

I arch a brow. "If I'd known it was that simple, I'd have cut that thing off days ago."

Harper chuckles and shakes her head. "I'm glad you didn't. I needed time...to work some things out."

She pauses and I get the feeling she's looking for, I don't know, permission to continue? Or maybe encouragement? "What things?" I ask.

If Harper's ready to open up to me, I'm here for it. The last couple of days without her have sucked. I missed her smile, her rule-following indignation. Hell, I even missed her snark when I was struggling to get my weak ass out of bed.

"There's something you should know about me." She toys with the hem of her shirt, unwilling or unable to meet my eye.

Worry tugs at my gut, but I ignore it. Whatever she has to tell me, it can't be that bad. And it sure as shit won't change how I feel about her. Harper's one of the coolest girls I've met. Not only does she totally get my HP references—Potterheads of the world, unite—she's not afraid to speak her mind or be herself. I love that about her.

Oh, shit.

"You have a boyfriend, don't you?" I ask, dread crawling up my spine. "Of course you have a boyfriend. I should've known. You're smart, beautiful—"

She presses a finger to my lips and my pulse thunders, roaring in my ears even as my cock stirs with interest.

Great. Because the only way to make this situation more

awkward would be getting a hard-on for someone else's girlfriend.

"I don't have a boyfriend, Chase."

Oh, thank Christ.

"So what is it, then?" I ask, relief tempered by curiosity.

Harper worries her bottom lip between her teeth. I take her hand in mine, squeezing it gently. "Whatever it is, you can tell me."

"You were right." The words are so quiet, at first I think I've misheard, because when has Harper ever admitted I was right about anything? "We have met before."

My brows slam together as I try to work out her meaning.

She takes a deep breath, her chest heaving with the effort. "At the Sig Chi party."

Realization dawns and I drop her hand, studying her face more closely as I try my damnedest to put the pieces of my broken memory back together. "You're—"

"Red," she finishes, nodding her head.

"But—"

Okay, maybe I'm in shock, because I can't seem to finish a sentence. None of this makes sense. It's insane. The odds have got to be...astronomical.

And that's why they call it fate.

Harper dips her chin and glances down at her hands, which are clasped in her lap. "I should've been honest with you from the beginning, but you didn't recognize me, and I was too afraid to tell you the truth." She straightens her spine and looks me in the eye. "I'm sorry. I just...I didn't want you to hate me, even if I deserved it. I was a coward."

"I can't believe it." I rake my hands through my hair. "All this time. You were right in front of me and I didn't recognize you." Disgust curls my lip. "Could I be a bigger asshole?"

"Hey, you've been through a lot with the concussion," she

says, resting a hand on my biceps. Her touch is light, soothing even. "You said yourself a lot of things about that night were fuzzy." She pauses, the corner of her lips twitching. "Plus, I didn't have my awesome red hair."

"I did like that hair," I admit, trying to process her words. "Wait. Why did you think I'd hate you?"

Harper flinches, and I'm immediately on guard. What else hasn't she told me? What else have I forgotten about that night?

"Because of...everything." She gestures to my leg. "You lost your scholarship because of me, Chase. I'm the idiot who told you to go up on that roof to get my shoe. If I hadn't, none of this would've ever happened. Because of *me*, you broke your leg, lost your scholarship, and are facing months of PT just to get back on your feet. How could you *not* hate me?"

I shake my head in disbelief. For a Ravenclaw, her logic makes zero sense.

How could she possibly think any of this was her fault? Or worse, that I'd blame her. It was an accident. One that could have been avoided if I weren't such a dumbass—as Coach so helpfully pointed out—but an accident, nonetheless.

"Harper, none of this is your fault. You didn't make me go up on that roof." I turn, taking both of her hands in mine. There's a sharp jolt of pain from my leg as I reposition myself, but I push through because there are bigger issues at hand than my comfort level. "I chose to climb that drainpipe because I was too fucking proud to walk away from a drunken dare. I was the idiot, Harper, not you."

The corner of her mouth twists and she pulls her brows low, wholly unconvinced.

"I admit I wanted to impress you. I was hoping to get your number." Still am, but we'll get to that part later. "But I didn't go up there because you told me to get your sandal. I went up there because I wanted to prove to those Sig assholes—to myself—that I was just as good as they are."

Her mouth falls open, forming a perfect O. "That's crazy, Chase. You don't have anything to prove to anyone," she says fiercely, passion blazing in her eyes. And damn if my chest doesn't swell with pride. This girl. How could she ever think I'd hate her? "You're one of the sweetest, funniest, most thoughtful guys I know."

"And I've got great legs," I add, winking at her.

"Your humility knows no bounds." A smile curves her heart-shaped lips as she reaches up to cup my cheek. Her fingers brush against my heated flesh and anticipation races down my spine, settling low in my gut. "The point is, you're a great guy and any woman would be lucky to have you."

"Even a Ravenclaw?" I ask, voice raw with desire.

"*Especially* a Ravenclaw." She holds my gaze and I see my own desire mirrored in her eyes, a white-hot need just begging to be unleashed.

I'm not sure which of us moves first. Hell, maybe we both do. One second we're making sex eyes at each another, the next our mouths are crashing together, a desperate mating of lips and tongues.

I've only known Harper for a week, but it feels like a lifetime as the dam of restraint comes crashing down. She tastes like coffee and chocolate and it just might be my new favorite flavor combination, because as her tongue slides against mine, there's no doubt I could do this all day. She's warm and soft, and I've been fantasizing about this moment from the first time she stepped into my hospital room with her killer curves and surplus of snark.

When we finally break apart—because breathing—Harper's cheeks are pink and she looks thoroughly kissed, if I do say so myself.

"So." She smooths her hair, and I can't help but notice there are a few more loose curls than when she first came outside. Although she looks adorable, I doubt Nurse Rogers would approve.

"So," I echo, inspiration striking. "If I want to keep my Prince Charming title, I need to do this right."

I grab my duffel from under the bench and unzip it. I dig around and find what I'm looking for on the bottom of the bag.

"Your right foot, milady." I affect my best British accent and gesture for her to put her foot in my lap. I don't have a clue if Prince Charming is British, but whatever, it's not like I'm being graded on historical accuracy. Harper giggles and kicks off her clog. Then she repositions herself on the bench so I can slip the sandal on over her sock. It slides on easily, and I do my best to buckle the little strappy things so it's somewhat presentable. "What do you know? It's a perfect fit, just like us."

Harper giggles again, and I swear I'll never get tired of hearing her laugh. "Is this the part where we run off and live happily ever after?"

"Not sure about the running," I say, glancing down at my leg, "but I have a good feeling about the happily ever after." I pull her in for another kiss and when her lips brush mine, I know I'm right where I'm supposed to be. I may have a long road to recovery, but I couldn't be happier than I am in this moment, holding Harper.

EPILOGUE

HARPER

Just one teensy tiny power nap. I shove my textbooks to the side and slump over the kitchen table, resting my forehead on my crossed arms. If I don't take a break, I'm going to go cross-eyed trying to read the sloppy, hand-written notes from my seminar. Besides, my brain is total mush. I doubt I could even spell NCLEX at this point.

Three hours of cramming like a madwoman will do that to a person.

Whose brilliant idea were mid-terms anyway? Talk about unnecessary stress.

And, as Bri helpfully reminded me before crashing an hour ago, finals will be here before I know it.

My only saving grace? Winter break.

It's not even Halloween yet, and I'm already counting down the days. Not just because it means spending more time with Chase, although that's definitely at the top of my Christmas wish list.

Right next to mind-blowing orgasms and four weeks of sleeping in.

#priorities.

Despite my enormous workload, the last few months with Chase have been incredible. His constant optimism and lighthearted spirit are the perfect counterbalance to my own *one-exam-short-of-a-nervous-breakdown* disposition. Proof—according to Bri—that opposites really do attract.

She's probably right because even now there's a hollowness in my chest that only Chase can fill.

Which is why I live for the weekend when I can drive up to Millheim and visit him. His parents have been great, but I'm pretty sure I'm not the only one looking forward to the day he gets that damn brace off so he can drive. The guy is not meant to be cooped up inside for long stretches of time, and with only physical therapy to keep him busy, he's been...restless.

Or, as his mother likes to say, ornery.

More like starts with an H and rhymes with ornery.

Heat pools low in my belly at the thought of Chase's calloused hands sliding over my body, his mouth claiming every intimate inch of me. The man has talents that extend well beyond the football field, which, as it turns out, isn't conducive to studying. Or napping.

Hardening nipples, on the other hand...

Knock! Knock!

I bolt upright and glance at the clock on the microwave. Nearly midnight. Who the hell is knocking on our door at this hour? On a Wednesday nonetheless.

There's another quiet knock, and I glance down at my thin t-shirt turned nightgown. *Spoiler alert:* it's doing nothing to hide the twin peaks. So, yeah, not really interested in answering the door as the braless wonder, but Bri's got an exam in the morning, and I don't want the idiot at the door to wake her.

College apartments are the worst.

Muttering under my breath, I make my way to the front door and press my eye to the peephole.

Safety first and all that.

A harsh fluorescent light illuminates the patch of cement outside the door, and under it stands a disheveled blond with the most captivating smile I've ever seen.

Chase.

What the hell? I throw the deadbolt and yank the door open. A frigid gust of wind whips around me, ruffling the hem of my nightshirt and raising an army of goosebumps on my legs.

"What are you doing here?" I demand, wrapping my arms around my midsection. Not that it does much good.

A crooked grin spreads over Chase's face, like the answer should be obvious. "I wanted to see you."

"No, I mean, how did you get here?" I lean forward and crane my neck toward the parking lot. No sign of Uber. Hell, there are no signs of life. All I get for my trouble is the familiar evergreen scent of Chase's aftershave intermingled with the cool fall air.

"I drove." The crooked grin morphs into a full-on, self-satisfied smirk as he holds up his right hand and twirls a keyring around his finger.

"You did what?" I whisper-hiss, poking him in the chest. Even with the crutches tucked under his arms and only one leg for support, the wall of muscle I call my boyfriend barely flinches. Which is both sexy and infuriating. "I thought you weren't supposed to drive with the brace on?"

I narrow my eyes and plant a hand on my hip for good measure. What can I say? The guy requires a firm hand.

Ideally on his backside.

"*Pfft.*" Chase waves a hand dismissively, the keyring tinkling like a string of bells. "I don't even need my left leg to drive."

Freaking football players.

I rub my temples, reaching for reason, which has clearly left the building where Chase is concerned. "So not the point. If you get in an accident—"

Chase's mouth descends swiftly, his soft lips devouring mine with the kind of focused determination he gives every aspect of his life. His tongue slides along the seam of my mouth and it doesn't matter what I was going to say, or whether he should be driving with the brace, because it's irrelevant. There's just me and Chase and the fire that burns so damn hot it could consume the sun itself.

I trail my fingers along his stubble-lined jaw, need coursing through my veins. I can't imagine a day where I won't want Chase with every fiber of my being, and despite his foolish actions, today is no different. I part my lips and he deepens the kiss. Each thrust of his tongue sends a shiver of desire down my spine, leaving me breathless when he finally pulls away.

And those goosebumps? Gone, thanks to the searing heat of his touch.

"I missed you." He rests a forearm against the doorjamb and leans into my personal space. Athletic shorts hang low on his hips—the guy never seems to get cold—revealing a sliver of the flat, defined ab muscles that always set my pulse thrumming. "Can I come in?"

"I'm studying," I return, lifting my chin. I mean, *of course* I want him to come in so I can ravage his body, but I'm not about to encourage him. Not when he broke the doctor's orders to get here.

Even if it was sweet of him to surprise me.

"I'll help you study." He wiggles his brows suggestively. "I'm really good at anatomy."

"Don't be gross." I swat him on the biceps, which he completely ignores, reinforcing the fact that despite my own solid build, I'm slight by comparison. Most kickers are thin and wiry, but not Chase. He's thick and, okay, all around delicious.

A fact he's well aware of.

He chuckles and the low rumble hums across my skin. "You didn't think it was gross last night when I—"

I clap a hand over his mouth before he can finish that sentence. "*Shh!* Bri will hear you."

"Babe. I hate to break it to you," he says, pitching his voice low, "but I'm pretty sure she knows exactly what goes on in your bedroom." He knocks on the crappy wooden doorjamb, and a hollow echo resounds through the still night. "These walls are thin as hell, and you make the most glorious noises when I'm licking your pussy."

And…cue the flaming cheeks.

Because, yes, even after two months of dating, I still flare up like a sunspot when he talks about sex. Or his cock. Or going down on me.

"Get your ass in here before I change my mind." The chances of that happening are approximately zero, but he doesn't need to know that, does he?

"Such a romantic," Chase teases, maneuvering past me, his crutches practically a natural extension of his body. "By the way, have I mentioned you're cute when you're embarrassed?"

"Once or twice." I roll my eyes and close the door behind him, throwing the lock. The motion causes my t-shirt to slip down off my left shoulder, revealing a swath of pale skin and a whole lot of collarbone. "But don't think flattery is going to get you out of trouble."

"Oh, I don't plan to use flattery." He turns and white-hot need flares in his eyes as he drinks in the miles of bare flesh not covered by my t-shirt. I should feel raw and exposed, my every imperfection laid bare, but it's not like that with Chase. With him, I only ever feel cherished. "I had something much more effective in mind."

"Oh?" I arch a brow in silent challenge.

"Come over here and let me show you." His words are rough and thick with desire. I know exactly what he's thinking—because I'm thinking it too—and when he gestures for me to move closer, I'm powerless to resist.

The need to feel his hands on my body is too strong, too primal, desire coiling low in my belly at the mere prospect of his touch.

Chase doesn't disappoint. When I step within reach, he lets one of his crutches fall to the lumpy couch and snakes an arm around my waist, pulling me flush to his body. The hard ridge of his erection presses against my belly, and I know that whatever he's got planned, I'm a goner.

"I plan to use my mouth," he says, planting a gentle, open-mouthed kiss on my exposed collarbone. "And my fingers." He rubs the sensitive spot at the small of my back, earning a quiet moan of approval. "And my cock," he finishes, rolling his hips so his length glides across my belly with the kind of friction that promises imminent pleasure.

Yes, please. Dibs on the kicker.

"Is that all you've got?" I choke out, the words a breathy whisper.

Who am I kidding? What he's offering is way better than studying, and we both know it. But it's about more than sex with Chase. Yes, he's been rock solid as I navigate clinicals and exams and study groups, but he's also been an endless source of support, laughter, and confidence.

Hell, the man believes in me even when I don't believe in myself.

I hate that he's still suffering the consequences of that stupid dare at Sig Chi, but I can't imagine senior year without Chase at my side. When he gets that brace off and he's ready to return to campus, I'll be by his side every step of the way. Because no matter what life throws at us or how challenging the circumstances, we've got each other. And if I've learned anything these last few months, it's that staying apart is a hell of a lot harder than being together.

Chase's hand moves from the small of my back, sliding over my curves until it's tangled in my hair. He lowers his forehead to mine, and my breath hitches in my throat. "Let's go to bed, Harper."

I smile, basking in the warmth of his embrace. "I thought you'd never ask."

∼

CHASE

THE BEDROOM DOOR closes with a soft snick, and Harper turns to face me. Her cheeks are flushed, but she's never looked more beautiful. A faded Hunger Games t-shirt hangs off one shoulder, her hair loose and tousled around her shoulders. Togas and nursing scrubs are all well and good, but as it turns out, I'm a sucker for these nerd girl tees.

Who knew they could be so sexy?

Not me, that's for damn sure.

Harper strides toward me, all long legs and confidence. Moonlight spills through the open blinds, slanting across the worn carpet and illuminating her every move. I sink down on the edge of the bed, making myself comfortable on the fluffy purple duvet, and spread my thighs to make space for her.

Christ, she looks good enough to eat.

My cock clearly agrees if the growing tension at the base of my spine is any indication. I'm so fucking hard and the mesh fabric of my athletic shorts is doing nothing to mask my erection.

When Harper reaches the end of the bed, she leans down, pressing a deep, bruising kiss to my lips. Then she fists her hands in the hem of my Wildcats sweatshirt and pulls it over my head in one smooth motion, before discarding it on the floor.

"I've missed you." I caress the smooth skin of her thigh. She's soft and warm, heat rolling off her body. "Missed this."

"It's only been three days." She flashes me an amused smile, but I don't miss the way her voice trembles. Or the way her thighs quiver at my touch.

"Feels like three months," I return, slipping my fingers in the waistband of her underwear and dragging them down slowly.

Harper laughs and threads her fingers in my hair, scraping her nails over my scalp. "That's because you have the sex drive of a jackrabbit."

I drop her panties to the floor and grab her ass cheeks, cupping them with my palms. "Are you complaining?"

"Not in the least." She strips off her t-shirt and tosses it to the floor, all her curves on full display. The woman has the most perfect tits I've ever seen. They're full and lush with these dusky nipples that are just begging to be sucked. And if it weren't for the fact that her pussy was level with my mouth, that's exactly what I'd do.

But the temptation to taste her is too great, my need for her too strong.

I angle her hips toward me, lean forward, and lick her right up the center.

She gives a delicious moan, tugging my hair as she throws her head back, lips parted with pleasure.

It's the most beautiful sight I've ever seen.

I may not be able to play football, but this I can do.

Hell, I live for these moments. When Harper lets her guard

down and it's just the two of us? When we can forget the rest of the world and lose ourselves in one another? There's nothing like it, and I wouldn't trade these moments for the world.

Harper spreads her legs a bit wider, giving me a perfect view of her pussy. She's hot and wet and it's all I can do not to throw her down on the bed and bury myself between her thighs.

"More, Chase."

The whispered plea breaks my trance. How long have I been staring at her pussy like an acolyte worshiping at the altar of orgasms and ecstasy?

Too long, judging by her desperate prayer.

With renewed focus, I lower my mouth and swirl my tongue around her clit, savoring the sweet taste of her flesh. She moans and leans into my touch, fingers raking over my scalp in silent command.

Harder. Faster. Deeper.

My cock grows impossibly hard as I spread her slick folds and slip a finger inside her tight channel. She sighs with relief, rocking her hips as I bear down on her clit with renewed fervor, desperate to give her the mind-blowing orgasm she deserves. She's been working her ass off at the hospital and studying for mid-terms around the clock. If anyone deserves a moment of unadulterated pleasure, it's Harper, and I intend to give it to her.

Hell, if I'm lucky, maybe she'll come twice.

"Yeeeessss," she moans, no longer worried about how much noise we're making. "God, yes. Chase, that feels so good."

I'm not about to quiet her, not when my name is on her lips, but maybe I should get Bri a pair of earplugs for Christmas.

Worry about that later, asshole.

Right. First orgasms, then earplugs.

A few more strokes and Harper's there, crying out my name as the orgasm rocks her body. Her knees buckle, but I hold her tight, stroking her gently as she rides out the aftershocks, a blissful smile on her face.

"That was—"

"Amazing?" I supply, winking up at her. "Incredible? Best you've ever had?"

Harper laughs and trails a finger down my cheek, her nail scraping against the scruff along my jawline. "Option D. All of the above."

"What can I say?" I shrug. "I don't do anything halfway."

Which is why, despite the hell that is physical therapy, I'm determined to get back on my feet, back on the field. It hasn't been easy, and the doc says it's only going to get harder when the brace comes off, but with Harper's support, and my family, I know I can do it. I have to do. So I can get my degree and start the next chapter of my life.

With Harper.

She grins and pushes me back on the bed. "I seem to recall you mentioning that once before."

Of course she does. The woman has a mind like a steel trap. "Now you have scientific proof that it's true."

"Technically speaking," she says, tapping a finger against her jaw thoughtfully, "I'd need more than one body of evidence to draw my own conclusion on the matter."

I gesture to my cock. "Experiment away."

When it comes to sex, I'm basically at her mercy and loving every minute of it.

"I think I will." She tugs my shorts down with quick, perfunctory movements. My cock springs free, standing at attention, but much to my chagrin, she doesn't join me on the bed.

Nope. She strokes my cock once from root to tip and sashays over to the nightstand, leaving me high and dry. It's all good though, because I get to admire her ass while she fishes a condom out of the top drawer and tears it open.

What can I say? The woman has a great ass.

When she returns, she climbs onto the bed, straddling me between her thighs as she rolls the condom over my length. Then she leans forward and kisses me, clearly determined to prolong this experiment—which is starting to feel like torture because my balls are so tight it's a wonder they haven't exploded—as long as possible.

Harper's tits are pressed to my chest, our bodies lined up in all the right places as her lips graze mine, her tongue skating over my lower lip in quiet exploration. The kisses start off gentle, but grow more daring, more desperate as she deepens them, rolling her hips and creating glorious friction where our bodies join.

I need to be inside this woman so bad it hurts, but with my leg in the brace, she's in complete control.

Thankfully, her need is as desperate as my own.

She positions my cock at her entrance and, with one swift move, she's seated herself to the hilt. She feels so damn good, I nearly come on the spot.

"Jesus, Harper. You feel incredible." I dig my fingers into the soft flesh of her hips as she begins to move. The tension at the base of my spine has reached a crescendo, and this woman is my only hope of relief. She throws her head back, dark hair cascading over her shoulders in loose waves, the delicate line of her neck exposed in the dim moonlight.

She's quiet for a long moment, the only sound the steady slap of our sweat-slick bodies coming together as one. When she finally meets my stare, her eyes are hooded with lust. "You say that every time."

"And I'll continue to say it every time, because it's true." It's always like this with Harper. No matter how many times we've been together—no matter how many times I worship her body

—it always feels like the first time. "You're a goddess. I knew it the first time we met."

A bead of sweat slides down her temple, and I reach up to brush it away with the pad of my thumb.

"Touch me, Chase." She bites her lip, never losing her rhythm. "I need you to touch me."

"Like this?" I lick my salty thumb and press it to her clit, tracing slow, steady circles around the sensitive bundle of nerves.

Harper moans in reply, and I accelerate to match her pace, desperate to feel her come apart one more time.

She's so fucking gorgeous when she's riding my cock. Not a care in the world as our bodies crash together, every last inch of me buried inside her as we barrel toward release.

"I'm so close," she pants, her rhythm becoming hurried and erratic as she chases the indescribable high that can only come from great sex.

My own orgasm is close and when it slams into me like a three-hundred-pound linebacker, my hips buck off the mattress, every nerve ending in my body humming with the most intense pleasure I've ever felt. And just like that, Harper's flying over the edge with me, eyes wide, the most glorious smile etched on her face as she shatters into a million tiny pieces.

Afterward, as I lay with Harper in my arms, her head resting on my chest, there's not a doubt in my mind that I'm the luckiest sonofabitch on campus. How I managed to get this girl is still a mystery to me. Hell, there are days I'm afraid she'll wake up and realize she can do better, but that's the old me talking. The one who always felt he had something to prove, who worried he'd never be good enough for an incredible woman like Harper.

A woman who—at this very moment—is skimming her fingers over my abs, the featherlight touch riding the line between pleasure and pain as she stimulates my hypersensitive, post orgasm nerves.

"I was thinking," she says slowly, as if choosing her words carefully. "If you don't have plans for Thanksgiving, maybe you could come home with me."

I freeze, every muscle in my body stiffening.

The silence is so deafening I'm sure Harper can hear my heart slamming against my ribcage as I descend into full-blown panic.

"If you want to," she adds hastily, the little swirling motions she was making with her hand coming to an abrupt stop.

Going home with Harper would mean meeting her parents. I've never met a girl's parents before. This is a big step. Shit. What if they hate me? Or think I'm not good enough for their little girl?

I glance down at Harper, taking in the dark tendrils of sweat damp hair that frame her sweet face. They'd probably be right on that count.

"Was this all part of your master plan?" I tease, stalling for time to collect my thoughts. "Seduce me with your feminine wiles and then ask me when I'm at my most vulnerable?"

She gives a haughty little snort and lifts her head so she can look me in the eye. "You're the one who showed up at my door in the middle of the night looking for a booty call."

"Booty call, huh?" I flash her a wicked grin. "If that's what you think, next time I'm going to show up wearing a trench coat and nothing else."

"I'm sure it will look great with your leg brace," she fires back, smirking.

"Low blow," I growl, tickling her ribs and earning a squeal of laughter.

She tries to roll away, but it's no use. We're tangled in the sheets, and I've got her locked firmly in my arms. There's no escape, not for Harper. But since I'm not a complete prick—and I really don't want to wake Bri—I pinch her ass playfully and pull her in close, relishing the press of her soft curves against my body.

Harper bites her lower lip, the tender flesh plumping around her teeth in a way that has my cock stiffening. It doesn't matter how many times I make love to this girl, I'll always want more. Need more. She's smart and funny and no matter how tough my recovery has been, she's been by my side, the calm to my chaos. "So, about Thanksgiving?"

I may be terrified of meeting her parents, of disappointing them, but if she needs an answer to that question, I'm doing a shit job of showing her how I feel.

So tell her, dumbass.

I cup her chin, forcing her to look me in the eye. For weeks I've been dancing around this moment, not exactly sure what to say or how to say it. The incessant tug in my gut pushes me forward, because I never want to see uncertainty in her eyes or hear it in her words. Not when it comes to us. "I love you, Harper Payne. There is literally nowhere else I'd rather be on Thanksgiving than at your side."

A slow flush spreads over her cheeks, barely visible in the moonlight, but her eyes shine bright and when she speaks, my whole world narrows to this moment, to the words I need to hear. "I love you too."

Warmth floods my chest and I swear to God there are fireworks behind my eyelids when I close my eyes and pull Harper in for a kiss, every nerve ending in my body sparking at the rightness of those words. Her lips are soft and pliant, melding to my own with the kind of languid passion that says she's all in. That there's no need to rush. Not when we have we have today, tomorrow, and all the days that follow to make our own happily ever after.

If you enjoyed Chase and Harper's story, one-click Claiming Carter, the first full length novel in the Waverly Wildcats series to find out how the Wildcats tackle the unexpected loss of their kicker!

www.jenniferbonds.com

ALSO BY JENNIFER BONDS

Waverly Wildcats

Holding Harper

Claiming Carter

Catching Quinn

Scoring Sutton

Protecting Piper

The Harts

Miles and Miles of You

Not Today, Cupid

Royally Engaged

A Royal Disaster

Royal Trouble

A Royal Mistake

The Risky Business Series

Once Upon a Dare

Once Upon a Power Play

Seducing the Fireman

ABOUT THE AUTHOR

Jennifer Bonds writes sizzling contemporary romance with sassy heroines, sexy heroes, and a whole lot of mischief. She's a sucker for enemies-to-lovers stories, laugh-out-loud banter, over-the-top grand gestures, and counts herself lucky to spend her days writing swoonworthy romance thanks to the support of amazing readers like you!

Jen lives in Pennsylvania, where her overactive imagination and weakness for reality TV keep life interesting. She's lucky enough to live with her own real-life hero, two adorable (and sometimes crazy) children, and one rambunctious K9. Loves Buffy, Mexican food, a solid Netflix binge, the Winchester brothers, cupcakes, and all things zombie. Sings off-key.

To connect with Jen, visit www.jenniferbonds.com to sign up for her newsletter and be the first to know about new releases, giveaways, and exclusive content! You can also find her on Facebook, Instagram, and TikTok @jbondswrites.

Made in the USA
Middletown, DE
05 February 2025